Second Chance
Book I, Cold Spring
By Nancy Henderson

MW00907515

Copyright 2016. Nancy Henderson.

Like my books? You can be notified of additional books coming out by signing up for my mailing list at my website:

http://www.always-a-story.com

Thank you!

To second chances…

Second Chance
By
Nancy Henderson

Chapter One

"Who is this again?" Samantha Stone plugged one ear as she pressed the other to her cell phone.

"Ian Woods" came the voice at the other end of the line. "Burt Tuttle gave me your number. He said you're taking over Jean's place and it needed some work. I've done a number of jobs for Jean in the past and know the property pretty well."

Sam listened to the rough voice at the other end of the line as the Amtrak train she rode on clicked and rocked rhythmically. The phone connection was poor, but not so much, that she couldn't notice the ruggedness in the caller's voice. An unexpected warmth radiated through her.

This couldn't be the same Ian Woods from school. The wild, unpredictable boy who she had crushed on all through elementary and junior high, then in high school…he had broken her heart.

He must be a good contractor if Burt recommended him. Burt Tuttle, Aunt Jean's significant other, was someone Sam would trust with her life if need be. Even if he were sometimes wrong, Burt always had the best intentions behind his actions. Still, Sam was mildly irritated that Burt had volunteered her money like that. Especially if the guy was that Ian Woods.

Ian went on about the pipes needing rework. Sam listened and politely thanked him, told him she'd have to get back to him, then hit "end" on her cell. She leaned her head against the window of the Amtrak as she watched the New York City skyline fly by. Doubt plagued her like a nagging toothache. Would this end up being the worst mistake of her life?

She tried to concentrate on the magazine that lay open in her lap but failed miserably. She would miss her Manhattan office on Sixth Avenue, as she would miss the lights, the noise, and the pulse of the city. Not that she partied, mind you. If she went to bed past nine o'clock without a stack of contracts to draft or manuscripts to read, it was considered a late night. New York was paradise for anyone who liked to be surrounded by books, authors, and the business of publishing, and that was what Sam had devoted the last ten years of her life to. Up until now.

She was leaving the city life behind for Cold Springs, the town in which she grew up. Coming home permanently was something she never thought she'd be doing until six months ago when Aunt Jean had died of an unexpected heart attack. They said her aorta had ruptured, that death had been instant and nothing could have saved her. Aunt Jean had passed doing what she loved, working in the little diner, the business she'd built from the ground up.

And now it belonged to Sam.

No one could have been more dumbfounded about it than Sam. Aunt Jean had left her everything, right down to the silverware and the tiny "Welcome to Jean's" custom coffee coasters. Sam didn't have a clue how to run a business, much less a coffee shop. Her restaurant experience went only so far as to order a large espresso at the coffee stand on her way to work each morning and the occasional cheese omelet on Sunday mornings when she allowed herself to stop working. The first thing she'd done was hire a lawyer, which she planned to see right after leaving the train. He had the keys and the final paperwork.

Despite being fairly happy in the city, she missed small town life itself. The quaintness the beach by Lake Ontario where she escaped as a kid and a teen, and despite having troubled relationships with Mother and Theresa, she found it strange in the city not being able to count on anyone witnessing her life as it were. Thoughts of Chet Tyler came to mind. She tried to push them away, but the hurt remained constant, even though there was nothing she could do about it. Chet had thought she was crazy for going through with this move. He had told her to sell the diner, get what she could from the sale, and buy herself something nice with the money. It was the only sensible thing to do as far as he'd been concerned.

Chet was always talking about what was sensible.

He never wanted their relationship to move forward, had insisted it was just fine the way it was. Maybe it had been fine, but Sam couldn't help but wonder that if the relationship was solid, would she have really even considered moving back to Cold Springs in the first place. She supposed that was the part that hurt, that there had never really been anything solid in their relationship.

She dozed off and on and gradually woke to the realization that Syracuse would be coming up shortly, which was where she needed to get off. Syracuse was approximately thirty-five miles south of Cold Springs. Memories flooded back to her. Saturday afternoon trips to the city, of going to the mall or the crowded farmers' market to buy flowers or vegetables. How long had it been since she'd last visited?

She'd flown to Aunt Jean's funeral but hadn't taken time to visit her mother or Theresa, her sister, just made it to the last ten minutes of the graveside service, enough to say a final goodbye and get back on the plane. Mother had a fit about that, as did Theresa. It was to be expected. But Sam had a full schedule that week, and she was upset enough as it was.

Guilt came fast and unforgiving. Sam hadn't come back or visited her family in so long. It wasn't due to hard feelings, but because she was simply too busy. Being part of Hodkins and Hochberg Literary Agency was no easy task. She had worked her way up from administrative assistant to senior literary agent in ten years. It was a feat she was more than proud of. It was her identity. Work was her whole life, her vibe. Her colleagues promised to hold a position for her in case she wanted to come back. For that, she was eternally grateful, but she also did not want to come back tail between her legs and have to work her way back up the ladder. Plus people would talk. They would think her a failure. She didn't want that either.

She simply couldn't fail. Ever.

Syracuse was announced as the upcoming stop. Sam closed the magazine still in her lap, slipped it in her laptop bag, and stood.

Syracuse had not changed, she noticed as she watched out the windows. People bustled about outside like fire ants. In the distance was the baseball stadium and The Regional Market. Sam exited the train as quickly as possible and spied Burt Tuttle waiting for her. Just looking at him brought memories of Aunt Jean.

Burt and Aunt Jean had never married or lived together, both claiming they were too set in their ways for commitment, although Sam surmised it had more to do with Social Security and pensions than independence. Burt stood waiting, dressed in his usual jeans and beat-up red flannel shirt, leaning against a blue Ford Ranger. He checked his watch, looked around as if he were in a hurry and wanted to be anywhere but here in the city.

She ran and caught him in a hug. "Hi, Burt. It's so good to see you."

"Why didn't you fly?" He took her bags. "Only cheapskates and bums take the train."

"Flying makes me nervous." Sam had never been comfortable flying since 9-11. She had not been directly impacted by the tragedy, but it had shot fear straight in the heart of every New Yorker just the same.

"You need to get a car if you're going to stay here," Burt said. "Something good in winter. You didn't forget how bad winters are up here, did you?"

Sam hadn't forgotten. Northern New York winters were hardly forgettable. Cold Springs had the double advantage of being located in the foothills of the Adirondack Mountains where the elevation was higher, plus it received lake effect snowstorms off Lake Ontario. However, economically, Cold Springs thrived off the winter tourists with snowmobiling, snowshoeing, and ice fishing.

"I've already set up a lease." She hopped in the passenger seat of Burt's truck. "I got a small SUV."`

"When?"

"Last week. Over the Internet."

"The Internet?" Burt shook his head, put his key in the ignition, and started the truck. "You can't order something like that over the Internet. How do you even know if it has good tires?"

"I already did, and it's an SUV."

Burt just gave her one of his disgusted looks combined with an eye roll. "When do you pick this fool thing up?"

"Right after you take me to the dealership." She smirked and was met by another look. "Then I have to go to the lawyer to pick up the building keys, and after that I'm a Cold Springs resident."

"Jean would be real proud of what you're doing."

Sam reached over and squeezed Burt's hand. Jean's death had taken a toll on Burt. She could see it in his face. He was half a person without her. Probably always would be.

"Ian Woods called me," she said to break the silence.

"Oh, he called you, did he? Good."

"No, not good. I know you're trying to help, and I appreciate that, but I rather you didn't give my phone number to strange men."

"Ian's not a strange man. I've known him for years. And you're going to need him. The place needs work."

Sam could tell Burt was getting upset, so she dropped the subject and went on talking about incidental subjects like the weather. She wondered how impossibly difficult it must have been to have to clean out Jean's possessions. Personal things like her clothing. Guilt stabbed her again. She should have come up to help him, not left him alone to do all that. She hadn't even helped Burt make the funeral arrangements. How could she ever make that up to him? She didn't know if she even could. Burt drove her to the dealership where she picked up her SUV. After convincing him she would be all right to drive the rest of the way to Cold Springs, he left her there and went home. Four hours later, and now not only physically exhausted but mentally as well, Sam stopped at her lawyer's office to finalize paperwork and collect the keys to the property. It was late afternoon by the time she was finished, and she was hours behind the self-imposed schedule she'd set for the day.

Thank heavens the drive to Cold Springs was uneventful. Not that she expected any problems. Cold Springs was a one-horse town with zero possibility for expansion. There was talk of dissolving the town due to the lack of businesses left, but as far as she knew nothing had been decided yet. However, if one wished to get away for a weekend or retire to peace and quiet, Cold Springs was perfect. Sam had no regrets growing up there. It was a town where everyone knew each other and had left her with fond memories. However, there had been no room to become a professional there or anywhere in the vicinity of such a small town. No ladder to climb and the only hard work came from farming, something she knew nothing about. It wasn't personal. Cold Springs was just not a place where she could reach her dreams. It had nothing to offer her. Until now.

Sam got off the highway and drove down Main Street. Aside from the post office, Aunt Jean's diner was the only establishment in town. Houses filled up the remaining part of downtown Cold Springs. It was a cute, picturesque little town, really, with trees lining each side of the street. The leaves had now turned brilliant shades of reds, oranges, and yellows, making it seem like a piece of stationary.

She pulled to the curbside and stared. Memories rushed back, cruel and bittersweet. A two-story brick building, Jean's Diner stood right next to the railroad tracks. Sam recalled with sadness how the dishes would shake in the cupboard when the train went by. Weeds grew by the door and grass poked up through the cracks in the sidewalk out front. The sign still hung on rusty hinges over the door, reading Jean's Diner, Best coffee anywhere. Aunt Jean had only been gone fewer than six months, but the place looked as if it had been deserted for decades.

Anxiety built in her throat. How stupid was it to take on a business she had no experience running? Her life had always been so calculated, right down to what she was eating for dinner.

She swallowed hard, struggled to push all negativity out of her mind. Getting out of her SUV, she pulled the diner's key from her purse. The key jammed in the lock, but her hands were shaking badly. With a slight amount of force, she opened the door.

The smell of stale air hit her as soon as she entered. The place looked exactly the same as she remembered. The ruffled yellow and white curtains with chickens imprinted on them. The red plastic booths lined one side of the room. Some of the plastic was torn and repaired with silver duct tape. Sam couldn't remember exactly when she'd last been here, but strangely, it seemed like yesterday. Any minute she expected Aunt Jean to come bursting around the corner, telling her to sit down, that she must be hungry.

She made her way through the kitchen and back storage room then upstairs to the tiny apartment Aunt Jean had lived in for over forty years. She opened the door and stepped back in surprise. It was as if Aunt Jean were still alive. All of her possessions were here. Her lamps, books, the furniture. Sam hurried to the closet and opened the door. Her clothing hadn't even been cleaned out. Burt hadn't done anything. Certainly clearing out her things would be personal, no doubt painful, but she would have thought he'd had asked someone to do it.

Sam touched the apron hanging on the back of the closet door and felt tears well up. Grease stains dotted every corner of the fabric. Well used, just like Aunt Jean had hung it here after a long day. Everything was here, her presence, her spirit.

Everything but Aunt Jean.

Guilt hit Sam with the force of a tractor trailer. She didn't want to be the one to throw out Aunt Jean's things. Maybe Mother would help her. Aunt Jean was after all, her sister. No. Nothing good would come of that. If Mother had wanted to help clear away Aunt Jean's personal affects, she would have offered to do so six months ago. Mother and Aunt Jean may have been sisters, but the two were as different as night and day, and mixed as well as oil and water. Mother still held animosity for her deceased sister, likely always would. Exactly why, Sam really didn't know. Sam had never pried, had just supposed it was simple sibling rivalry as she felt between herself and her own sister, Theresa.

Sam would have to clean out the apartment herself. Aunt Jean had left the place to her, so the responsibility fell on Sam, no one else.

And she would bring the diner back to life. There was no other choice.

~ * ~

Ian Woods split a chunk of Scotch pine in half with one blow of the ax. He stepped back, leaned the splitting maul against the stump and wiped the sweat from his brow. A cool breeze tugged at the tail of his flannel shirt as he finished the last of his water. It would certainly be easier to get through the twenty cord of wood with a splitter, but he didn't mind the hard work. Every scream of his biceps cried freedom, and it tasted too good to take for granted.

He watched as a cloud of red-winged blackbirds flew overhead already grouped and ready to head south. Dying for a smoke, but trying to quit, he breathed as deeply as his lungs would allow, held it until it felt as if his chest would burst, and slowly exhaled. He had a feeling winter would be early this year. Not just talk of it on weather reports. He could feel it. Already the air was filled with the smell of rotting leaves — some had turned and already fallen — and the air had a coldness like the first frost would be just days away. He was glad to get a jump on splitting Burt's firewood. He would need it soon.

Beauty, perfection, peace. Being able to go outside whenever he wanted was still foreign, and he wondered if he'd ever get used to it, ever take it for granted again.

He was probably nuts to come back to the town where everything happened and everyone knew about it and gossiped about him, but Cold Springs and its landscape were in his bones. He'd always planned to make a life here, create a contracting business and raise a family here. Despite his grave doubts, he still held that dream, and he wanted to see if he could do it.

An image of Sam Stone appeared in his head. First the gangly, rail-thin girl with the round wire-rimmed glasses, always with her nose in a book then the high school girl who made the glasses seem dangerously sexy. The whole librarian thing suited her. He wondered if she was still pulling that off. He felt like an idiot after calling her this morning. There had been no hint of recognition in her voice. Just total surprise, maybe even a little annoyance. Of course, he was nothing more than a stranger to her.

Burt said she'd moved downstate to the city and was a big hotshot publisher or something. No doubt too good for the likes of this town.

He'd been hoping that she'd remember him and take him up on his offer to maintain the diner for her, maybe arrange some regular paying gig where she'd set up a maintenance contract with him to take care of the place, maintain the boiler and air conditioning system. If he could get a few opportunities like that, he'd be set for steady income to start his business.

Did Sam know about his past? All she had to do was get a background check on him so there was no use lying if she asked him.

He didn't have much time to get his business to turning over a profit, as his parole officer had pointed out at his last meeting. If he didn't start proving that he could support himself financially, he'd have to find a regular paying job, and who the hell would hire an ex-con?

~ * ~

The pale blue-and-white-trimmed Victorian stood at the corner of Lee and Town Streets in the heart of Cold Springs. Her mother's home. Not the home Sam grew up in. That had been lost in an ugly and complex divorce. Mom had bought this place five years ago after her books took off. She'd used a down payment solely from her royalty checks on her writing. A feat Sam found both amazing and intimidating for an author who wrote strictly for small presses and did not receive monetary advances. In Sam's line of work — past line of work — her clients needed advances to survive. That told you the sheer volume of books her mother sold on her own.

Sam pushed that aside and knocked.

"Door's open."

"Hi, Mom."

"The spare room is upstairs on your left," her mother called from the kitchen. "You can put your things in there."

"I thought it was to the right," she answered. Sam didn't have any belongings. She had made it distinctly clear that she was staying at Aunt Jean's—her own place—now.

"Oh, I converted that room over to a media room."

Sam hadn't remembered that from the last time she'd visited. Of course, the last time she'd been to Cold Springs had been last Christmas, and Mother had been on deadline so she'd felt like she was staying alone. Sam understood what it meant for a writer to have deadlines, but she was also her daughter.

She glanced at the wide, sweeping oak staircase. Mother had done a lot with the place, papering the walls in floral wallpaper typical to the period in which the house was built.

She walked down the hall toward the kitchen, by a room at the foot of the stairs and stopped. The door to Mother's writing room was open. Sam hadn't seen it in years. Guilt hit her fast and hard. She had visited the offices of her author clients on occasion but couldn't remember the last time she'd seen her mother's. She stepped inside.

A monstrous desk engulfed much of the room, and an equally huge computer monitor sat on top of it. Posters of her book covers covered most of the wall space, clinch covers of men and women posed in various compromising positions; books all bearing titles with the name of body parts in them. Mother's pen name, June Alibaster, was displayed on all of them.

Mother didn't use a pen name for the most common reason authors used pen names, to distinguish between genres so readers would not be confused or disappointed. She wrote only one genre: erotic romance. Sam wondered if deep down Mother was ashamed of what she wrote. If she didn't want people to know what she wrote, why didn't she write something less risqué? But of course, Sam knew why: money. Erotic romance was one of the biggest selling genres of all time, and writers could make a decent living from it.

Sam noticed a framed award on the far wall. "June Alibaster, Best Erotic Series." Sam was surprised. She knew her mother was prolific, and she knew her books sold well, but as far as being well written...Sam had never read one of her mother's books.

Sam should be ashamed of herself. Was she really that uptight that she couldn't read eroticism? Her agency didn't represent it, but she could have certainly seen what kind of stories her mother wrote. Maybe it had more to do with not wanting to read about sex derived from her mother's imagination…?

She went out and found her mother in the kitchen. It was a gourmet kitchen, totally remodeled with granite countertops and every appliance a cook could dream of. Ironically, Mother rarely if ever cooked. She just simply wanted the best of the best.

Styrofoam containers scattered the kitchen island, along with plastic utensils and paper towels. "Hi, Mom."

Madelaine Stone looked much younger than sixty-four. Her hair was dyed deep auburn and cropped high above her shoulders in the latest fashion. She wore casual but classy dress: tan capris and sandals, a white-ribbed tee with a light sweater over it.

"Hello, Samantha."

Guilt pierced Sam as she searched her mother's face for a hint of longing but found none. Perhaps she hid it well. Sam wondered if she should move in for a hug but decided against it. Aunt Jean never had hesitations with hugging. With Mother, you were always left to wonder. Sam didn't understand how two sisters could be so different.

"I thought I'd just do sandwiches." Mother rushed around the kitchen like a sparrow. "The grocery has a new remodeled deli area. There's plates over there. Your sister will be here any minute."

Speaking of differences. Theresa lived three houses down from Mother in another Victorian house with her three daughters and lawyer husband, Shawn. Theresa and Mother shared coffee every morning and spoke often. Mother never failed to mention it to Sam.

Sam tried not to feel resentful, but it was difficult. Theresa had been homecoming queen, had married her high school sweetheart, captain of the football team, had given Mother three gorgeous grandchildren, who were now all getting straight As and excelling at sports. What was not to love?

Sam dished a portion of potato salad and helped herself to a turkey sandwich on a Kaiser roll. She wondered if the meal would be suitable for Theresa because it wasn't fancy.

As if on cue, she heard her sister's minivan pull up. Since she lived three doors down, Sam wondered why Theresa drove instead of walked, but she guessed walking was likely beneath her. Sam's two nieces, Maggie and Justine, and nephew, Michael, piled in the house, banging the screen door on the front porch.

"Hi, Grandma!"

Mother hugged them all at once. They quickly scattered, each knowing the way around the house like they'd been there often. One of the girls stopped, stared at Sam.

Sam crouched down to meet her at eye level. "Hi, Maggie. How are you?"

Maggie looked scared. She looked around for her mother.

"Can you say hi to your Aunt Samantha, honey?" Theresa's voice was more command than question.

"Hi, Aunt Samantha" came Maggie's robotic response.

"Kids, come say hi to your aunt."

Each child filed in, giving Sam a peck on the cheek, each greeting just as mechanical as the next. Guilt hit her, and she wondered if they would be so stoic if she had chosen not to move so far away. Or if she'd come to visit more often.

"They'd know you better if you had more contact with them." Theresa gave her a quick peck on the cheek. And there it was. Thanks, Theresa.

"How are you, Theresa?"

Theresa sighed. "Oh, you know. Running the kids here and there. Who has time to do much else? You're looking good. Of course, you have time to take care of yourself, having no kids or husband."

Sam ignored the backhanded compliment. Theresa was always full of them, always pointing out what she assumed was wrong with her life. "How's Shawn?"

"Doing very well. He's about to make senior partner at his firm."

Sam pasted a smile on her face. Shawn Maxx, Theresa's gorgeous, successful, wealthy lawyer husband was doing very well. Of course, he was. How would he be doing anything but? Anyone in Theresa's life was always doing very well.

"And your sister's president of the PTA now," Mother said.

"That's great."

Theresa smiled and helped herself to a stack of plates from the cupboard.

"There's paper plates on the counter." Mother gestured.

"We don't use them." Theresa cut her off as she placed the pre-made turkey sandwiches on each plate. "It's not good table manners. Kids! Lunch is ready."

One by one, her children filed in. "I don't like turkey."

"Me, neither."

"I bought paper to save on dishes." Mother's tone was annoyed.

Theresa looked at her as if Mother had lost her mind. "I'm not having my children raised like animals."

"By eating on paper plates?" Sam broke her silent vow not to get involved.

"Oh, like you'd know how to raise kids." Theresa snorted.

Maggie wrinkled her nose. "Mom, turkey's gross!"

"So is potato salad," Justine chimed.

"Well, just...hold on. Mommy'll get you something else." Theresa rushed around like a chicken with her head cut off. Sam was exhausted just watching her. As if she owned the place, she opened every cupboard until she found a jar of peanut butter. She then grabbed a jar of jelly from the refrigerator. "Don't you have anything but marmalade?"

"I think there's some apricot preserve left in the door."

"I want grape jelly!" Theresa's youngest, Mike, screamed at an ear-splitting decibel.

"I'm getting it, honey."

"Grape jelly!"

"Apricot?" Theresa stuck three-quarters of her body in the fridge. "Who eats that stuff?"

"I happen to like it on my bagels." Mother made no move to assist in the search for grape jelly.

"I'm not eating apricot or marmalade!" Maggie folded her arms across her chest.

"Grape jelly!"

Theresa emerged from the refrigerator with both jars of marmalade and apricot spread. "You're going to have to make do with what Grandma has. Maybe next time she goes to the store she'll remember what her grandchildren like to eat."

"Nooo!" With that, Mike threw himself on the floor and proceeded to display the most violent fit of temper Sam had ever witnessed. Theresa picked him up as he flailed and threw his head back, raging and wailing. "Mikey, please. Be a good boy for Mommy. Please eat like a nice boy, and we'll go home and watch any movie you want today, okay?"

"How come he gets to choose?" the girls started in.

"Because I said so!" Theresa snapped as Mike's hand came down hard across Theresa's face.

"Mikey, please. Now eat nicely and we'll watch a movie later, okay?"

"PB and Js on fine china." Sam couldn't help it. She met Theresa's look of scorn with a wide smirk.

Sam held her sister's glare as long as possible but was the first to look away.

They sat down at the table.

"So you're taking over Aunt Jean's diner." There was that look on her face, like Theresa thought it was a crazy idea.

"I am."

"How are you going to do that?"

"I have a lot of work ahead."

"That's putting it mildly." Theresa cut her sandwich with a knife.

"You're right. It is a lot of work." She'd already submitted her business plan and got the startup loan she needed to stock the diner and do minor repairs. Plus she had rolled her 401K over to an IRA. She didn't want to touch it, but it was there if need be.

"Aunt Jean was a wonderful person, God rest her soul, but she was no businesswoman. She didn't have a clue what she was doing."

"She ran it for over thirty years," Sam was quick to defend. "I should think she had some idea what she was doing."

"Yes, and she barely scraped by. She never had a vacation her entire life."

"Maybe she didn't want one."

Theresa laughed. "Who wouldn't want or need a vacation?"

Sam did her best to maintain composure. Theresa and Shawn went to a five-star resort every winter. Mother told her about them every year.

"Don't get mad, Sam." Theresa touched her arm. "All I'm saying is that you should have thought this through. You don't know the first thing about running a business. I don't want to see you fail, but frankly, I can't see anything else happening with this."

"She can get her old job back," Mother added.

"Well, that's good, at least."

Sam hated that she felt the need to defend herself. "I won't need to get my old job back. I will make this work. You'll see."

This time, Theresa placed both hands on her arm. "If you want to come back to Cold Springs permanently, I think that's great. I'd love to have you close by. We all would. I just don't see this diner as a viable prospect. You could get yourself a nice office job in the city and commute. That would be a whole lot less stressful. Don't you want less stress?"

Sam wanted to ask Theresa how she knew what amount of stress she could handle, but she held her tongue. She hadn't finished her sandwich yet, but she suddenly felt full and threw the container in the trash and stood. "I'm going back to the diner and do some work."

"So soon?" Mother asked. "You just got here."

"Well, like I said, I have a lot of work to do. It's not going to get done by itself."

"Why don't you do the sensible thing?" Theresa called to her as she made her way out the door. "Sell the place and share the money with us."

Sam stopped cold in her tracks. Mother and Theresa had inherited nothing from Aunt Jean's estate. Aunt Jean had left everything in her bank account to Burt and all her possessions and the diner to Sam.

Sam couldn't deny that the situation was awkward at best. Sam would have thought Aunt Jean would leave something to Mother, being that they were sisters. And to Theresa? Perhaps Aunt Jean was like the majority and thought Theresa already had everything. Nevertheless, perhaps Sam should have fought the will, demanded that the diner and all Jean's possessions be sold at auction and the proceeds split evenly.

But she hadn't. She wanted this diner. She wanted to make a new life here in Cold Springs where everyone knew everyone and people could be trusted.

And she wanted to think the best of her family. Even Theresa.

Silently, she let herself out and went back to the diner.

CHAPTER TWO

Sam's blood was boiling by the time she got back to the diner. The more she thought about her perceived obligation to sell the diner and split the money with them, the more irritated she became. She had every single right to inherit this diner. It was what Aunt Jean wanted. Theresa and Mother hadn't even spent any time with her. Like the time she came down with pneumonia, who had been the one to fly all the way back here and take care of her? Not Theresa and Mother, that was for sure.

Sell it and split the money with them! Theresa had to get the last dig in. Every. Single. Time. Sam didn't know what it was about her sister that angered her. Maybe because she was the favorite in their mother's eyes. Sam had grown up under the scrutiny of a mother who expected both daughters to be track stars or homecoming queens, and when Sam didn't deliver…Theresa rose to the top. Maybe that's why she never read her mother's books.

Letting herself in the front door of the diner, Sam had trouble shutting it again and had to body slam it to get it to line up correctly to be locked. She'd have to hire a contractor to take a look at that.

She remembered the man who had phoned her cell earlier. Ian Woods. If Burt recommended him, he was probably reliable. Maybe she shouldn't have given him the cold shoulder. It was just that all she could think of was the Ian Woods she'd gone through school with. How embarrassing would it be if he turned out to be one and the same? Facing him after his rejection, even after all these years, would still be humiliating.

Sam could still recall every detail of that night so long ago. She'd saved for months to buy a prom dress, and rehearsed for weeks how she would ask Ian to accompany her. She'd almost passed out when he'd said yes. Just thinking about it brought back a rush of nerves. She waited hours for him to come by and pick her up. Theresa laughed it up when she found out Sam had been stood up. She'd reiterated that the whole thing had been set up as a joke on her, that someone like Ian Woods would want nothing to do with the geek girl brainiac.

Despite all the years that had gone by, if Ian Woods was one and the same, Cold Springs was awfully small, and it was almost inevitable that they would cross paths, especially when she reopened the diner.

Bypassing the kitchen that seriously needed cleaning, she hurried upstairs to the apartment. Mother had offered her spare bedroom if Sam wanted to stay there while she fixed up the upstairs apartment. Sam appreciated the offer but had refused. Living with Mother, even temporarily, especially with Theresa always intruding, was not going to work. She shouldn't feel so irritated, but she couldn't help it. Those two fed off each other and had a perfect way of pressing her buttons, even if they didn't mean to. This was why she seldom came home to visit…and now she was here for good.

She let herself in the apartment and shut the door. All the walls were painted white and were still in fairly good condition despite the dust. Built-in shelves and drawers lined one side of the one-room apartment. She stared at the salt and pepper shakers of various sizes and shapes which cluttered the shelves. Aunt Jean's customers were always giving her shaker sets over the years. She had some from Cancun, a pair of slot machine shakers from Las Vegas, even a set replicating the Great Wall of China that a customer had given to her upon returning from a business trip overseas. The memories were too close, offering no place to run.

There was an attic crawl space. She could box everything up and temporarily put Aunt Jean's things in there for a while. At least for now so she wouldn't feel so guilty, not as guilty as she would if she got rid of everything.

She stepped into the bedroom. Aunt Jean's bed was made. A single twin bed. Photos of friends at the diner lined one dresser. There was another of her mother when they were little. By the nightstand were framed photos of various sizes of her and Burt. They looked so happy together.

Sam had no right removing any of these things without Burt's permission. She thought about calling him, but it seemed too personal and felt she should do it in person. She quickly hurried downstairs, eager to be away from Aunt Jean's personal things. It was like she were still alive up there. Like Sam was intruding.

Which was certainly a problem Sam hadn't foreseen. She had thought living upstairs would be fine. Just an empty apartment she could make her own. She hadn't expected it to be so alive with a living memory of everything that was now gone.

Perhaps coming home had been a mistake. Tears stung the back of her eyes as she jumped in her vehicle and backed into the street. She didn't belong here. Were Aunt Jean alive, she'd have the right words Sam needed to hear. She'd fix things, or at least reassure her.

It hadn't taken more than five minutes to reach Burt's house, a small ranch with a separate two-story detached garage. Dusk was quickly settling. Sam hadn't realized that she'd spent so much time at the apartment, but she had spent more time than expected picking up her car and even more at Mother's and admitting she was now exhausted was an understatement. She shouldn't have come here tonight.

Burt had every light in the house on, which was odd considering he usually worried about conserving electricity.

She turned her vehicle off and hopped out, knowing Burt never bothered locking his door. She didn't knock, just let herself in unannounced. Knowing Burt, he would scold her for knocking, saying she wasn't a guest, that only strangers knocked.

Sam heard talking and stopped in her tracks.

"Did you meet her yet?" Burt asked

"No, and I don't intend to."

"Why not?"

"What's the point?" came the familiar voice. It was not Burt but the voice that had called her from the train. Ian.

It was rude and presumptuous to just barge in here and assume Burt had no one over. No one had been parked in his driveway.

"Look," came Burt's voice. "Every man's got to have somebody."

Was he talking about Jean?

Sam backed up, started to leave when she felt something move under her foot. A cat yowled, nearly scaring the wits out of her. Burt and his guest came running.

"Uh, hi. Sorry about the cat. I uh, stepped on him…or her." She looked around, but the cat had run off. "I hope he's okay."

"He's all right." Burt waved his hand. "C'mon in and sit down. You remember Ian?"

Ian. That Ian Woods. Of course, it was the same Ian. How many Ian Woods did she think lived in Cold Springs? Sam smiled probably the dorkiest smile she could muster. Yup. Just like being sixteen again.

He wore jeans, ripped at the knee, and a white T-shirt. His face—five o'clock shadow—had a chiseled jawline and thick, dark hair that hadn't begun to recede yet. And his eyes, the same ice blue as when he was seventeen. Only he wasn't seventeen. He was older. He looked different. Serious.

Sam backed up against Burt's refrigerator.

"Hi, Sam."

"Hi" was all Sam could mutter. Gone was the boyish grin. She expected some sort of sarcastic remark from him but was relieved when none came. Ian was just unusually quiet. Deathly quiet.

Burt was headed toward the living room. Sam stopped him before he could disappear. "I can't stay. I just wanted to ask you about Aunt Jean's things."

Burt turned toward her, his expression troubled. She felt as if she'd said the wrong thing and felt immediately guilty. "What do you want to do with everything?"

"It's your place now." He turned and continued on to the living room. "I've got TV to watch." His tone was sharp. Avoidance. That was why Aunt Jean's things were still there. Sam should have known. Of course, she'd known. What else had she expected?

"Well, maybe I'll just box things up," she called into the living room. "You can go through them when you're ready, okay?"

"Dammit, I told you, they're not my things!" Sam jumped back, feeling as if Burt had slapped her. Rarely had she heard him swear…well, except when there was a punchline attached to it. He'd certainly never sworn at her. She realized where it had come from, that it wasn't Burt, but grief talking, but it still hurt.

Sam started to leave, realized that Ian's gaze was on her and tried to avoid making eye contact. "Well, I suppose I could take her clothes to a thrift store or something."

"We can put them in the back shed." Ian motioned toward the back of the house. He caught the door as she opened it and followed her outside. "What are you doing tomorrow?"

"Tomorrow?"

"I'll have time in the morning. I'll help you box and load up everything. We can use my truck."

Ian's voice was like warm chocolate, and Sam felt warmth rush to the pit of her stomach. Sam was both shocked and surprised by his eagerness to help. She wondered how Ian had gotten to know Burt. Sam had known Burt her whole life but she'd never known Ian to follow in Burt's or Jean's lives. The only place Sam had ever known Ian was from school.

She wondered how Ian's life had unfolded since high school. Obviously, he hadn't left Cold Springs which was a fine path to take with his life, although she couldn't help but feel a little envious, which was stupid.

She didn't even know where that had come from. No one had forced her to leave Cold Springs or forced her to lose touch with the people she grew up with. She only had herself to blame for that.

"You don't have to do that."

"No, it's okay."

"You barely know me."

"I know Burt." He was quick to answer. "I know he wouldn't want Jean's things thrown out, and I know he certainly thinks a lot of you."

Sam didn't see any point in arguing. She needed the assistance, and Ian was right. Burt wouldn't want Jean's things thrown out. Maybe in time he would want to go through them himself. If they were stored in his shed, he'd have his own timing and he'd have no rush to do it. Maybe it would make things easier on him.

"All right. Tomorrow then, if you're sure it's no trouble."

"No trouble at all."

"Okay, well. Thank you."

She got in her vehicle and drove back to the diner. All the while, she wondered how odd it was that someone would offer to help when they barely knew her. Plus there was nothing in it for him. No one ever did anything like that in the city.

Of course, Cold Springs had always been friendlier than New York City. That was one of the reasons why Sam wanted to come back. There was no personality in the city. Nothing was personal. Here everyone had their nose in everyone's business, and while it was often annoying, sometimes it was just…nice. In the ten years she'd been away, Sam had missed nice. Nice felt good again.

It was dark by the time she let herself in and made it back upstairs to the apartment. She had every light turned on and it still didn't feel right. She was an intruder here. On one hand, it was as if Aunt Jean would come around the corner any minute and welcome her with open arms into her home, and on the other hand, Sam was an intruder and had no right messing around in Jean's things, moving and rearranging — certainly not taking her things to Goodwill. Even though Aunt Jean had left everything to Sam, it still felt wrong.

Shoulders slumped, she looked around the room. There was no way she was sleeping in Aunt Jean's bed. Not that she had died in it. Sadly, Aunt Jean had suffered her heart attack while talking to the customers she loved downstairs in her diner. Nevertheless, Aunt Jean's bed was too personal. The entire bedroom made up the way it was, was too personal. She would sleep on the loveseat in the little living room.

Making sure the door was locked, she kicked off her shoes, quickly changed into yoga pants and a T-shirt, and found a blanket and extra pillow in the top of a closet in the hallway. She had expected the most sleepless, uncomfortable night of her life with her feet hanging off the end of the loveseat. She fell asleep as soon as her head hit the pillow.

~ * ~

True to his word, Ian's truck was waiting in front of the diner first thing the next morning. He drove a beat-up Ford F-150, an older model with rust taking over much of the blue paint.

"Thanks for offering to help." Sam held the door for him. The breeze had a brisk chill to it, sending cold straight to her bones. She would have to shovel the sidewalk this winter, she suddenly thought. The thought was an unwelcome one.

"It's no problem. I wasn't doing much today."

"How do you know Burt so well?" she blurted as he passed by. She decided the only way to know was to bluntly ask. That and she felt a bit overprotective of Burt now that she was back in town, or maybe now that Aunt Jean was no longer around. Or maybe a combination of the two.

Ian shrugged. "I started going to the diner before…before I left town."

Sam got the distinct feeling that Ian didn't want to talk about it. She didn't know why, just something she picked up on. "Can I get you some coffee?"

"No, thanks." He went to pull the door shut and the knob came off in his hand. "Well, that needs to be fixed."

Sam gave a surprised start.

"Good thing you know somebody." He flashed her a cocky grin. "I'll get my tools."

Sam hadn't seen him smile before, and it suited him. Not just suited him. It lit up his whole face. He was rough and brawny like one of the heroes in her mother's romance novels. Sam felt heat rush to her cheeks.

She stood in the kitchen as he left and came back with a toolbox. "So you became a handyman."

"Contractor."

"Sorry… What's the difference?"

"Handyman doesn't sound very professional." He winked. "Sorry about your aunt, by the way."

"Yes, well…thank you. I appreciate that."

"I think you'll make a go of it here," he said, his voice husky, deeper than she remembered.

She smiled. Ian was the first person besides Burt who believed in her. Even if he did want her to hire him as her handyman. She'd take it.

"Are you sure you have time?" She didn't want to take him away from anything he needed to do. "Can I pay you for your trouble?"

He seemed hesitant for a minute then scratched his head. "Burt said you know a lot about contracts?"

"I used to I suppose. Why?"

He pulled a piece of paper from his back pocket. "I was wondering if you'd be willing to take a look at this and see if it's legit."

He handed the paper to Sam. "It's a maintenance contract I was just offered. My first one. I've never really dealt with them before, and I really want to sign it, but I'm not sure about some things in it. Could you take a look at it and let me know what you think? I'll pay you, of course."

Sam briefly glanced at the document. She didn't mind returning the favor for Ian, but a maintenance contract and a book contract were two entirely different animals. "I really don't have any experience with anything other than publishing contracts."

"It's all the same legal bullshit, right?"

"Well, perhaps, in some way, I suppose." She really didn't know without studying it. "Can I take a day or two to look it over?"

"Sure. No problem."

She set the papers on the counter. "I'll start it tonight and see how it reads."

"That'd be fine. Thanks."

"You're welcome." Sam was grateful for the opportunity to do the favor. She felt better doing something for him, like she wasn't beholding to him. Sometimes she hated that independent streak in her that felt she had to return every favor someone gave her. Years of living in the city, she supposed. Here in Cold Springs people just did things for others because they were being nice, not because they were trying to gain something in return.

The next five hours went by in a blur. Ian and Sam said next to nothing to each other. Ian did as she instructed, boxing things up, lifting boxes, throwing them in his truck and taking them over to Burt's back shed. He made twelve trips and refused to take any money Sam offered to pay for the gas he used hauling the boxes. When he left, she felt guilty for moving all of Aunt Jean's possessions, exhausted, and also relieved. Now, standing in the little apartment, it was exactly as she had expected it to be before moving here: empty except for the loveseat and the little kitchen table.

Her suitcases sat on the floor by the table. Hoisting one onto a kitchen chairs, she unzipped it and proceeded to unpack. It really wasn't that bad. When she had time, she would repaint the place, maybe in various shades of blues or greens, but now she just wanted to make this a real home. A real home was a little closer now, but still far away with her furniture in storage. Pulling her cell from her back pocket, she dialed the moving company. She had programmed the number into the phone before she left New York. Thankful for preplanning, she got them on the phone and instructed them to bring everything to the second floor of her building as soon as possible.

Sam had stored her furniture and large belongings in a storage facility she supposed as a safety measure in case she had to go back. Now she was determined to make a go of this place and cut a life out for herself in Cold Springs. Something about her mother and sister implying that she would fail had set the decision for success in her. That was enough to convince her that she was in this for the long haul. There was no going back.

Now as she looked around the little empty apartment, she felt herself become a little more at ease. She didn't own much, nothing more than one person living alone for so many years would own. She had Ian remove Aunt Jean's bed to make room for her own when it arrived with the movers, and she planned to make do sleeping on Aunt Jean's loveseat that she decided to keep. It wouldn't be the most comfortable thing to sleep on, but she could manage for a day or two. She felt herself relax somewhat. It would feel like home soon. She wondered if Aunt Jean would approve.

~ * ~

Sam had offered to pay Ian Woods for fixing her front door, but he'd refused to take any money. When she'd asked him what she owed him, he'd said the door was just a sample of his work. Now, even as she worked scrubbing the dining room — she still had yet to tackle the kitchen which was the worst and most dreaded task at hand — she still couldn't stop thinking about him. She had stayed up late reviewing the maintenance contract he'd brought over, and it really wasn't terrible. Although it could be better, were Sam in Ian's shoes she'd really try to renegotiate it.

She wondered if he had a family, a wife, kids. With looks like that, he most definitely must have a girlfriend. His life was none of her business, but she couldn't stop thinking about him. There was something very different about him now. It was like a totally different person in the same body — only a much more mature, sexier body.

People generally as a rule did not change. Something or someone must have had a major effect on him to bring about such a one-eighty in him.

She thought of her apartment in New York. Life in the city suddenly seemed so simple. In New York, all she had to worry about was her work and her comfortable apartment. She didn't have to worry about what Ian Woods thought of her. Here…everything was just—

Small towns were just awkward.

A knock came at the door. Sam could see Burt through the window. She opened the door, thankful that people couldn't just walk in at will now.

"Hi, Burt."

"Mornin'." Burt looked around the dining room as he entered. "The place looks nice."

"I haven't done anything to it yet."

"That's what's nice about it. Looks exactly the same. Where's the coffee?"

Sam smiled and pointed to the right of the counter where customers would sit. "I thought I'd put the coffeemaker there."

He perched himself onto one of the high counter stools. "Well, where is it?"

"It's on order."

Burt turned and looked at her as if she'd just sprouted horns. "You mean to tell me you own a coffee house and you don't even have a coffeemaker? What'd you do with Jean's?"

"It wasn't working. So I ordered another one. A bigger one, so we can serve even more coffee." Sam smiled, thinking she'd finally won Burt over with the promise of a never-ending supply of coffee.

Burt gave her that look that screamed disapproval. "I could have looked at it for you. You probably didn't have it plugged in."

"I plugged it in." Sam went back to cleaning.

"What am I supposed to do now? I came here for coffee."

"Um...we don't open for another week."

"We? Who's we?" He pointed to the yellow mug on the counter. It now contained lukewarm coffee. "Where'd you get that?"

"I made it." She smiled.

"With what? That newfangled coffeemaker that's on order." He made air quotes with his fingers.

Sam tried not to laugh. It was good to be back around Burt's humor. It made her feel welcome and wanted here — in a strange sort of Burt way. He was eccentric and kind and was the model of small town and big hearts, just like Aunt Jean. Seeing him was the closest thing to having Aunt Jean here with her now. "It just so happens to be instant coffee. Can I get you some?"

Burt made a face. "You're going to be running a place that serves coffee and you try to kill me with instant? I'd rather go without."

The door suddenly opened and Mother and Theresa came in. Both were dressed in stylish matching tan linen slacks and fuchsia tees with matching cardigans.

"You two look alike," Sam said. She wondered where they were off to. Always somewhere.

"We're having our portraits done," Theresa answered. She looked around and frowned.

"For a book event?" Sam asked.

"No, it's just something we planned." Mother waved her hand as if it were nothing. "Long before you came back. Burt."

"Madeleine." Burt folded his arms over his chest.

"I expected to find you here." Mother's dislike was obvious. "There's no bringing Jean back by wasting time here."

"Wow, that's harsh."

"Well, you act like she's the only family you ever had."

Sam knew the remark had cut, and she was surprised when Burt remained silent. There had never been kindness between Burt and Mother. In Mother's eyes, Burt had never been good enough for Aunt Jean. Or maybe he was too good. Sam didn't really know the cause of their animosity toward one another. It wasn't her place to know.

However, since becoming a resident of Cold Springs, Sam didn't think she'd have a choice but to know, unfortunately.

"We were just going into the city and wondered if you needed anything."

Theresa went to one of the windows and touched the yellow chicken curtains. "You're not keeping these are you?"

"Until I get something new," Sam answered. Tacky curtains were the least of her worries at the moment.

Mother whipped a notepad and paper out of her large handbag. "Curtains," she muttered to herself as she counted each window. "We'll stop by the mall."

"I thought you were going to reupholster the booths." Theresa wrinkled her nose to exemplify her distaste.

"I plan to when money starts coming in." Sam tried to hide her irritation. She didn't want her mother picking out her curtains any more than she wanted Theresa's decorating ideas. Jean's wasn't a place people came to for atmosphere. It never had been. People came for hot coffee and hearty, home-cooked food, which was what Sam intended to give them. Eventually, she planned on replacing the less-than-pretty things like the booths and the cracked tile in the bathroom, but it could wait until she was making a profit. Now was not the time.

Mother adjusted her purse onto her shoulder. "Jean never cared what the place looked like."

"Jean worked damn hard here." Burt spun around. His arms remained folded across his chest, his angry gaze on Mother.

"I never said she didn't."

"See that you don't."

Mother sighed. "My sister never had a knack for décor. That's all. She did work hard here. Too hard. I don't want to see my daughter working herself into an early grave like Jean did."

"I'm used to hard work, Mom." Sam appreciated her mother's concern. Being a literary agent was hard work, but it was different. Sam surmised she was in for a surprise once the reality of running a restaurant kicked in, but she looked forward to the challenge. It was a much-needed change of pace and a chance to carry on Aunt Jean's legacy.

Remembering Burt's coffee, she went to the stove behind the counter and lit the burner to heat up some water. Nothing.

"Darn."

"Not working?" Burt asked.

"What?"

"It was just a minute ago when I made my coffee." Sam filled a cup of water and stuck it in the microwave to heat. "I'm afraid your coffee won't be the best this morning, Burt." She glanced toward her mother and sister. "Coffee?"

"It's instant." Burt smirked. "Better run."

Mother adjusted her purse. "We've got to be going."

"That's too bad." Burt chuckled.

Sam sighed. "I'll call someone later."

"Call Ian," Burt said. "He's local and he's good. Won't cost you an arm and a leg."

"Ian Woods?" Mother and Theresa said the name with the same unbelievable tone.

"No," Theresa snapped.

"Absolutely not." Mother agreed.

"Ian paid his dues." Burt spun around in his chair, his tone heavy with the same defense he held for Jean.

Sam sat down at the counter. "What do you mean 'paid his dues'?"

"He murdered someone!" Mother proclaimed. Sam nearly choked on her coffee. "Right in cold blood."

"Who—"

"I don't know. Does it matter? He's a murderer."

"That's not what happened, and you know it." Burt shot her a venomous look.

Sam thought for a moment. As an agent, she'd read countless murder mystery manuscripts. Like books, real life always held two sides to the story. "Maybe it was an accident."

"It was no accident," Theresa said.

"Does it even matter?" Mother asked. "He's not trustworthy."

"He's more trustworthy than you," Burt shot at Mother.

"You can't talk to my mother like that," Theresa said.

"I just did, and nobody was talking to you anyway."

With that, Mother and Theresa stormed out.

"Don't worry about Ian. He's all right. You can trust him."

"What did Ian do to go to jail?"

"It's not my place to say, but he's a good man."

CHAPTER THREE

"Thanks, John." Ian extended his hand to John Taylor, co-owner of Hank's Lumber.

Ian had no doubt that John would have gladly returned the shake to anyone else. Instead, John glared at Ian's outstretched hand like he was a leper. Ian quickly pulled it away, emotions from humiliation to down right fury fighting for control.

The anger won, always. Anger was his protector. It made everything right when the world dumped on him. Justified things when life threw nothing but shit his way. It was his court, judge, and jury and it never discriminated.

They told him that he would get these reactions, and Ian knew he would, but it still did little to prepare him for small town life. Everyone had their nose in everyone's business. They always had, and it had never bothered him before now. Maybe it had been a mistake coming back to Cold Springs. His P.O. said he'd made the right move and that people would eventually get used to him. He'd told Ian that most ex-cons had a better chance of making it on the outside if they went back to their hometown near their family. He'd said acceptance and trust took time and he needed to be patient. A damn lot of time. Ian should be used to dealing with time.

Leaving the lumberyard office, Ian hopped in his truck, an old beater that Burt had landed from a vehicle auction for him. It had more rust than metal, and the bed was crooked, but it got him from point A to point B, and that was all that mattered.

He didn't know where he'd be if not for Burt. They had never been more than acquaintances before Ian's incarceration, but it was during his imprisonment that Burt had visited Ian. Burt had told him what the town was saying about him—which Ian surmised was a hell of a lot worse than Burt let on—and that he didn't blame him for what he'd done. Burt had been the only one to validate his crime, not that it was right, but the reasoning behind it. Burt had made him feel less of a monster, and for that, Ian owed him everything.

Ian had to find more clients if he was going to make a go of this business. Burt had told Ian's parole officer that he was Ian's employer, that he was backing Ian's business until it became financially sound on its own. The P.O. gave Ian three months to be making a solid profit, meaning each month he needed to be in the black which would have been damn near impossible without Burt's help with things like setting up, getting such an affordable truck and a place to stay, not to mention all the free meals he provided.

Still, the fear of failure always haunted him. He had won two construction bids just north of Watertown, far enough away where word of his past hadn't traveled, but he needed more clients if this business was going to survive long term. He drove down Main Street, seeing Jean's Diner. Part of him wanted to stop and see if Sam had read his contract yet, but the sensible part of him said to just leave her alone. She had his cell number, and she would call when she was finished with it.

Burt said she'd never married and had no kids. "No baggage" was his exact words. There was a time before prison when Ian couldn't understand the meaning of baggage, but now, to know the security of a warm and loving family waiting on your return after a long day of work...Ian could even fathom how good baggage must feel.

Sam Stone had certainly changed since high school, but so had he, and not for the better. Sam, however...she was no longer that gangly kid who had asked him to prom. The beanpole awkward girl with glasses was cute and sexy as hell, and where had those glasses gone? She must have contacts now.

He wondered why she had chosen to come back and what she hoped to gain by opening Jean's place back up. Maybe she just wanted to carry on her memory. He certainly couldn't blame her for that. The little diner had always been the backbone of this town. It was a place everyone gathered and talked about everything and everyone. That certainly wasn't likely to change. And you're not likely to find anything but trouble around her either.

Yeah. He didn't need any more trouble. He'd gone through enough for one lifetime.

~ * ~

Sam grabbed her cell phone from the counter. "Hello?"

"Samantha Stone?"

"Yes."

"This is Mike from We-Move-It Movers. We can't find your house."

The call took Sam completely off guard. They weren't scheduled to arrive until two days from now, but she needed her things and she was more than willing to make this work.

"We just drove the whole length of Main Street. We don't see an address."

"How about if I stand outside and flag you?"

"That'll work. We'll make another pass."

Sam hung up and went outside to wait for the movers. Excitement filled her. It would be good to have her personal things around again, would feel more like her. Not to say it wouldn't feel more like home because strangely being immersed in Aunt Jean's world was so like home it was almost surreal.

The October sky hung low with dark clouds threatening a thunderstorm. The scent of fall loomed in the air, rotting leaves and the smell of burning firewood coming from the chimney on the house down the street. This was what she remembered about Cold Springs, and it filled her with hope.

Half an hour passed with no traffic whatsoever. She called Mike again. "Hi, this is Samantha Stone. Where are you?"

"We're on Main Street. Where are you standing?"

Sam didn't understand. "I'm standing in front of the brick building. I don't see you."

"We don't see you either."

"Okay..." There must be some sort of mistake. She heard the sound of rustling paperwork coming through her cell. "601 Main Street, Cold Springs, Virginia. That's where we are."

Disbelief smacked her in the face. "Cold Springs, New York."

Silence on the other end.

"Doesn't your paperwork say New York?"

"Okay...well, this is a problem. We'll have to figure this out." More paperwork rustling.

"You're not going to double charge me, are you?"

"You'll have to take that up with the office, ma'am."

"But I distinctly said New York."

"We'll get back to you." The line went dead. "Hello?" Sam hit end on her phone and went back inside. She went straight to scrubbing the oven, eager to take her frustration out on something physical.

"Of all the stupid things…" Great. Now she was talking to herself. What next? If she started answering, she'd have real problems.

The one immediate action which would take her mind off her problems, she was quickly learning, was cleaning, and Lord knew she still had plenty of that to do, especially in the kitchen. Marching into the storeroom, she found a bucket, rubber gloves, and a box of scouring pads, and she thought she'd get a jump on the work ahead. She started on the grill first. The grill top was black with old built up grease.

She put on rubber gloves up to her elbows, grabbed her bucket and scouring pads. She didn't know how many hours had passed before she started to see the actual grill surface. Perspiration beaded her forehead and soaked her hair. She wondered when she'd last worked this hard outside of a gym. Funny, she would never need use of one now with all the physical work running this place would take. Not that Cold Springs had an actual gym anyway.

No matter, think of the money she would save. Satisfaction slowly surfaced as the grill top began to show through the grease. When she was finished, she got down on her hands and knees and proceeded to scrub the front of the grill. She scrubbed around a small stainless steel handle. Must be a utensil drawer or something. She tried tugging it open, but it wouldn't budge. Getting up on her knees, she used all her weight to yank on it. The smell hit her at the same time the drawer gave way.

Black slime went everywhere, spattering her face, the walls, the newly mopped floor. The drawer hit her chest, splashing the liquid all over her white T-shirt as she fell back into the cabinets behind her. She choked back a gag. The stench had to be close to that of a dead body. What the devil was this and why hadn't Aunt Jean ever cleaned it?

"Sam?"

Theresa of all people! "Don't come back here just yet."

Theresa hurried into the kitchen. "Oh my Go— What did you do?"

"I pulled on this drawer."

"That's a grease trap! Didn't you know that? Everyone knows that."

Theresa hadn't cooked a meal since getting married. Shawn had hired a nanny, housekeeper, and cook the first month of their marriage. As far as Sam knew, her sister still had the service.

Sam tried to stand but slipped in the vile ooze which congregated at her feet.

"You're never going to get that out of your hair. I'd give you the number of my stylist, but I wouldn't do that to her."

Sam stood, slipped on the grease, and fell, whacking her elbow on the floor."

"Are you okay?"

Sam didn't answer. She bit her top lip, trying to keep herself in check. "What can I do for you, Theresa?"

"I wanted to see how you were doing. Not so good as I can see."

"I'm doing fine."

"Mom was afraid this would happen."

"Oh, really? She was afraid I'd pull on this drawer and spray this shit all over myself?"

"There's no need for that kind of language." Theresa put her hands on her hips and stood there as if she were about to send Sam to a time out.

"I'm not one of your kids, Theresa."

"What's that supposed to mean?"

Sam grabbed the countertop and hoisted herself up. "It means I have a brain."

"Are you calling my children stupid? How dare you?"

"What? No, no I wasn't calling your children stupid. Don't be ridiculous."

"I'm not going to come here and be insulted. You know I didn't have to drop by. I was just trying to be nice to you. Mom said this would happen. I should have listened to her."

Sam tried not to let her sister's words hurt, tried not to picture Mother trying to talk Theresa out of coming over here, but it sounded exactly like something Mother would have said. Sam was certainly no expert at child rearing, but she couldn't understand why a mother wouldn't want her siblings to be close. It was as if Mother liked the fact that Theresa and Sam were distant. Mother had always been that way and Sam had never understood why. She sighed as Theresa turned and left.

Not two minutes had passed when Ian Woods was standing in the kitchen.

"What happened to you?"

"What's it look like?" she snapped. "I'm sorry. I'm having a bad day."

Sam regretted her words before they left her mouth. She had never remembered being this irritated in New York. Sure she'd had her bad days, but they hadn't been this bad. At least they hadn't seemed like they'd been this bad.

"What are you doing here?" she asked, suddenly very aware of her appearance. And his presence. She was totally alone with him. An ex-convict. While Burt wouldn't say what Ian had done, but hadn't denied Mother's accusations that he'd killed someone.

It didn't make any sense. Burt was sensible…somewhat sensible anyway. He may be a bit eccentric at times, but he wasn't outright stupid. If Ian was dangerous Burt wouldn't have anything to do with him. Ian was never a threat to anyone in school that Sam recalled. None of it made any sense.

Ian said something about a contract, but Sam wasn't paying attention. Contract? "Oh, right. I did look it over." She motioned toward the counter where she put it this morning in case he came by.

"I also wanted to see if the door was all right. That and Burt called me. He said you had a broken stove. Do you want me to take a look at it?"

Burt. He was trying to save her money again. He wouldn't put her in harm's way if he knew Ian was any sort of threat. Of course not.

She looked up at Ian who towered like a giant in the middle of her small kitchen. How had he killed someone? What had he used? A gun? Knife? His bare hands?

He didn't look dangerous. Tight jeans, work boots, five o'clock shadow, and hair tousled as if he had just climbed out of bed with some hot twenty-year-old.

Sweet mother! She shouldn't feel attraction to him. She should feel wary of him. Ian Woods wasn't the innocent, cocky jock from high school. He was now an ex-convict and could very well be dangerous. She should be worried about being alone with him.

But…something. Maybe just crazy senseless desperation to make it here. She needed her stove working if she was going to reopen the diner.

Sam cleared her throat. "Do you have the time to take a look at it?"

One side of his mouth turned up in a half-grin. Sam tried to get out of his way. She hadn't realized that she'd stepped in the grease pool until it was too late. Once she started sliding, there was no stopping. Worse than the fact she was already covered with grease or that she was falling was she was taking Ian with her. She didn't know who had grabbed whom first. Suddenly she was clinging to his shoulders and he had his hands around her waist as they both hit the floor.

Sam landed hard directly on top of Ian. She stared down at his stunned expression, her face less than an inch from his.

Man…those eyes. Blue, like a sexy Caribbean pool, just like Sam remembered.

"Oh!" She scrambled to get up. Ian's hand was still on her waist. "Are you okay?"

"Yeah." He released her.

Sam quickly rolled off him. "I'm sorry."

He stood, offered his hand to help her up. Sam accepted it. It was warm and strong and immediately set her heart pounding. She stood, started to slip, but he caught her around the waist.

"Um…" Step away, stupid! What was wrong with her? He was going to think she still had a thing for him.

But how could he not think it? Furthermore, how could she not fall for him all over again? He still possessed that thing, that something about him that attracted her to him in the first place. He paid his dues. Burt's words rang in her head. She stepped away. "I'm sorry. I made quite the mess." Gingerly, she stepped around him and got a rag and bucket of bleach water. "I'll get this cleaned up."

"I'll get my tools." He went outside and reappeared with a toolbox in hand. "Your orifice is probably plugged."

"Excuse me?"

"The pilot orifice."

"Oh. Right. Of course." Oh, Lord! Sam felt her cheeks flush. Of course, he was talking about the stove! As he leaned over, she couldn't help but stare.

"Hey, I wanted to tell you I'm sorry."

"For what?"

"For high school…everything. I was a bum kid. I didn't—I heard later how upset you were that I never showed up that night."

"No." She shrugged it off, suddenly feeling foolish for talking about a time so long ago. "It's fine. I went anyway."

"I didn't see you there," he blurted then looked down. "Yeah, I was a jerk."

"Who'd you go with?"

"Jane Benton," he answered.

Figured. Prettiest cheerleader in upstate New York.

"If it matters, I had a lousy time. Jane left with Frank Hanes."

"Mom said they married a few years ago." Sam crossed her arms and smiled. "Maybe you were their matchmaker."

"Maybe. So how did the contract look?"

Right. The contract. "For the most part, I think it's a good contract. However, I did find a couple of things. I flagged them with sticky notes. I don't want to touch it until I wash my hands, but you'll see the one I wrote where my suggestion would be to add mileage to your fee, assuming you'll be traveling quite some distance for this work since there isn't much opportunity here."

He seemed to think for a moment. "Yeah, that's a good idea. I'd be driving just north of Watertown so I would want to be compensated for gas and wear and tear on my vehicle, assuming I'll have a better truck soon anyway."

"Another point I thought worth mentioning was the clause in the third paragraph on the second page. I marked that as well. It says something about if you don't answer every maintenance call within thirty minutes you'll owe them a hundred dollars. That's something I'd want to negotiate since you likely wouldn't arrive before thirty minutes."

"That one did worry me."

She nodded, glad that he had noticed the clause. "You can always try to renegotiate. It can't hurt to ask."

"I will. Thank you for looking it over." His expression was sincere. "Not many people would take the time to help a stranger."

She smiled. Sam no longer considered him a stranger. Perhaps another strange enigma in this crazy small town and the bizarre turn her life had taken lately, but certainly not a stranger. What was even more bizarre was that she felt no sense of danger around Ian when all common sense told her that she probably should. Her gut told her she was perfectly fine.

"Anyway, I'd like to make up for it and thank you for your business. It hasn't been easy. I appreciate you taking a chance on my work. Do you like pizza?"

"Yes." A simple answer. The truth. Everyone liked pizza, didn't they? It was one of the staples of America, but...

She had no business going anywhere with him. She kept silent as she watched him work, tinkering with the little door on the front of the stove.

He reached over the grill and fumbled with one of the shutoffs by the wall. "Here's the problem." He turned the knob and it lit. "The gas has to be turned on. Each one of the gas cocks has to be on."

He showed her the pipework on the back. Sam nodded, feeling both relieved and incredibly stupid. She didn't even know enough to turn on the gas and she was trying to run a restaurant. "So you gonna let me buy you pizza, or what?"

CHAPTER FOUR

Sam fell into bed sometime after midnight. She should be used to these long days. Lord knew she'd spent enough sleepless nights reading manuscripts as a literary agent, but this was different. Working here was physical, as well as mental, which brought on an entirely new depth of exhaustion.

She needed sleep. Without sleep, she'd be crap tomorrow, but she had too much on her mind. Lately there was always too much on her mind. Would it ever end? Or would worry and anxiety become a constant companion in this new life? Aunt Jean had never seemed burdened by worry, but with someone like Burt in her life, how could she? A partnership like that was once in a lifetime and not to everyone's lifetime it seemed.

Rolling on her side, she pressed her face into the soft flannel pillowcase and closed her eyes. Thoughts drifted to Ian Woods. She still couldn't picture him being in prison. He had to have been jailed for something like cheating on his tax forms or something. Not that those things weren't bad enough. They just seemed…less criminal somehow.

Sam tried to recall the last time she'd been with a man. Too long. Not that any man hadn't given her anything but grief. John had been a huge mistake, but she hadn't listened to anyone's advice or any of the writing on the wall. Never date a coworker, and certainly, never sleep with one. It wouldn't work out because they were both workaholics, and when it went sour, things would be awkward, and it had been. Thankfully, John had left the firm a few months later. Sam still wondered if he'd left because he felt just as awkward as she had, but it didn't really matter. It was all water under the bridge now, and they'd never see each other again.

Then there was Chet. They still called each other often and it was…weird. Sam didn't really miss him, per se. Not like someone was supposed to miss an ex. Or at least someone who they once thought was "The One." She had simply stopped seeing him but still maintained contact with him by phone and text, but it was friendly, nothing more. Chet had given no hint of missing her and Sam, well, she was getting along fine without him. So what were they…really?

Pizza with Ian. Where would he take her? Someplace in the city, no doubt, which meant a thirty mile drive alone with him. Time alone with an ex-convict who could possibly be dangerous. And if he was not dangerous, she'd still be alone with him and have to carry on a conversation with him when they had absolutely nothing in common. Bottom line: Ian was sexy as hell and possibly a threat to her safety. And she couldn't wait to see him.

She should call him and cancel, make up some lame excuse.

She was just about to doze off when the phone rang, making her jump. She stared at the clock by the bed. Nearly 1 a.m. "Hello?"

"Reservations please."

"Excuse me?"

"Is this the Easy Rest Inn?"

Sam sat up in bed. "You have the wrong number."

The person at the other end of the line hung up. She lay back down, and the phone blasted again. "Hello?"

"Is this the Easy Rest Inn?"

"Wrong number again." She hung up.

She looked around the room, expecting the phone to ring again, but it did not. Too early to get up. Too late to make a cup of coffee.

Irrational thoughts and worries gradually ebbed to stillness as she lay
on the loveseat listening to the quiet, too quiet, of living in a tiny town. Now and then, a car would roll by, but other than that, complete silence.

She was just about to drift off to sleep when she heard something fall downstairs. Or outside. Which was it?

Another thump. It sounded like it came from the front of the building.

Throwing the blankets aside, she got up, grabbed her baseball bat, and raced downstairs. She tripped her way through the storage room, not turning on the lights for fear of being spotted, and peered out the window.

Burt. He stood by the door holding a large cardboard box. Sam watched as he looked over his shoulder. He put the box down on the sidewalk, picked it up, then set it back down again and peered over his shoulder. What was he looking for? Or was he making sure no one was watching him?

Burt adjusted the box a few more times then stepped away. Leaving it directly in front of the door, he walked down the sidewalk and disappeared around the corner.

Sam opened the door and peered out. She almost called to him but changed her mind. She looked down at the box. A funny noise came from inside. Scratching. Then mewing.

Barefoot, Sam stepped out onto the sidewalk. She opened the lid to find exactly what she expected. Two orange ears were illuminated from the glow of the nearby streetlight. The kitten couldn't be more than a couple of months old. The poor thing was probably scared to death, and here Burt was leaving it on her doorstep in the middle of the night like a crazy man. Maybe Alzheimer's had finally set in. She should be angry. Correction: she should be royally pissed right now.

She plucked the little ball of fur up into her arms, went back inside, and clicked on the lights. "Hi, little one."

The kitten started to purr.

Warmth curled in the pit of her stomach. Sam had never owned a pet before. Part of her had always wanted one, but animal ownership never fit into her lifestyle. For a person who was always working, never home, it didn't seem fair to leave a pet all alone most of the day.
She and Theresa owned a cat when she was little. Cats required litter boxes and bowls and certainly food. Sam didn't have any of those things, and it was the middle of the night.
Still holding the kitten, she pulled the box inside, both surprised and delighted to find every item for kitten care complete with litter scoop, food, and manual Congratulations on the Purchase of Your New Kitten in the box.

But now…she would still always be working, but now she worked from home. A kitten was the last thing she needed, and it was another responsibility in her life. She should really be angry with Burt, making the assumption that this was what she needed or wanted.

She rubbed her face in the kitten's fur. What was one more responsibility?

~ * ~

"I can't believe you let him in here!"

Sam poured her mother a cup of coffee. Mother took a packet of artificial sweetener from the little stainless steel box by the glass sugar container and poured it into her cup.

She sat at the counter, looking impeccable wearing black slacks and a turquoise colored silk jacket. She had an interview with a television station in Syracuse today. They were impressed that such a successful writer lived in the North Country. Sam was proud of Mother's accomplishments, and she wished she could tag along, but she had too much work to do in preparation for opening day. Not that Mother had invited her to go anyway. Theresa, however, had been asked to come…obviously.

"He didn't even charge me anything." Sam was surprised that she was so quick to defend Ian Woods. Tonight was pizza night, and she was a ball of nerves and anticipation.
 "You know what he's done!"

"Lower your voice, please," Sam whispered and motioned toward the back room. Ian was in the back repairing one of the coolers. She'd called him early that morning after having a truckload of supplies delivered, and one of the coolers wasn't working. She needed every cooler she had now. Sam was thankful he had time to squeeze her in.

"He's here?" Mother's expression was incredulous. "He murdered someone."

Mother leaned forward. "Promise me that you're done hiring him for anything. And stop listening to Burt. He's a nut job."

"He's fine, Mother."

"There are a lot of things you don't know about people in this town. I know you think you can take care of yourself what with living in New York all those years, but things are different here. I know you think you know everything coming from the city, but you've been gone a long time." Mother gulped down the last of her coffee and glanced at her watch. "I've got to go. Remember what I said about Ian Woods. I mean it."

"Good luck today, Mom."

"Thank you." She waved her hand and was off.

Mother wasn't gone two seconds before Ian appeared from the back room. "Thanks."

"For what?" She hoped to God he hadn't heard the entire conversation.

"You didn't buy into the gossip about me."

Sam shrugged, tried to hide her embarrassment that he'd heard her mother. Part of her did buy into it, and that part of her feared him just a little now. The other part, the rational side, knew she had a job to do and Ian Woods filled that need. "You're a lot cheaper than most contractors out there."

"I need all the money I can get. Look, if you don't want to hire me because of my past…"

"It's none of my business."

He nodded. "I appreciate that."

He was standing close, and Sam suddenly became very aware of him. She wanted to ask him if everything Mother said about his past was true. Prison for murder seemed very far-fetched, the stuff of novels, but if he did go up for murder, how come Burt said he could be trusted? Nothing about murder was trustworthy. "Burt says you're not a danger."

"You can trust Burt."

Sam looked down at her shoes. Worn tennis sneakers stained in stove grease and spaghetti sauce. As if on cue, the door opened and Burt came in. "Mornin'."

Sam hurried to get Burt's coffee, eager to get away from Ian. "Good morning, Burt."

Burt perched himself on one of the counter stools. "What's for breakfast?"

"Today's special is cheese omelet, home fries, and coffee." She winked. They weren't open for business yet, but she was willing to cook him breakfast. It would be good practice.

Burt gave a miserable look. "What kind of special is that? It's on the menu."

"I'll knocked fifty cents off."

"A special is something not ordinarily in the menu. It's special. That's why it's called the special."

Ian put his tools away and headed toward the door without a word to anyone.

"Ian, wait." Sam quickly poured a cup of coffee into a Styrofoam cup. "Take this with you."

"Thanks." He hesitated, holding her gaze. Sam's heart skipped unexpectedly. His eyes were ice blue, almost as if he wore colored contacts which somehow she doubted.

"Are we still on for pizza?"

His smile was infectious. "Sure, if you want. I'll give you a call."

Sam nodded, hoping Burt hadn't caught any of the conversation. Not that he wouldn't find out eventually anyway. When it came to gossip, Burt was about as prolific in it as her mother and sister.

When she turned toward him, he was grinning, but to his credit he said nothing. "Thanks for the kitten, Burt."

Burt grinned from ear to ear. "I don't know what you're talking about."

"Uh-huh." She poured herself a cup of coffee and took a slow sip.

~ * ~

Ian didn't know if he should call Sam or just show up. He paced the small second-story studio apartment he called home. It was barely six hundred square feet, but it was perfectly fine for him, and he felt lucky to have a roof over his head.

It was two rooms: one large space with a small row of cupboards and a countertop and sink to the left and a tiny bathroom with a small shower, toilet and sink. Burt allowed him to rent it for a hundred dollars a month. Ian knew the old man was cutting him a deal, and Ian vowed to make it up to him. Burt had been the only one to stand by him in this town. He was a friend when his family and those he thought were his friends had turned their backs on him. For that, Ian would be forever grateful to Burt.

Ian checked his appearance in the mirror. For God's sake, it was just pizza, but he had changed into the best jeans and T-shirt he owned. He didn't own many clothes, just enough to get by every couple of days before he had to do laundry again.

Running a comb through his hair again, he grabbed his keys and headed out the door. He hurried down the steep flight of stairs that snaked up the side of Burt's garage. Inside, he found Burt inspecting his truck.

"Problems?"

"This damn thing is making noise again." Burt pushed himself out from under the truck.

Ian grabbed his hand and hoisted him up. "I can look at it for you."

"No, I think I got it."

"What'd you do?"

"I put some more oil in her." Burt wiped his greasy hands on his shirt. "I put a quart in just about a day or two ago."

"Why don't you let me take a look at it?"

"Because you got things to do." Burt stepped in front of him, preventing him from looking under the hood. "Where you off to?"

Ian didn't want to tell Burt. He didn't like keeping things from him, but he didn't want Burt taking the pizza night between himself and Sam as anything other than appreciation for her business. Still, he could lie to Burt no more than he could believe in Santa Claus. "I'm taking Sam Stone for pizza. She hired me for a couple of jobs. It's the least I can do."

Burt's expression told him more than he wanted to hear. "You two would make a good pair. Sam's got a lot of Jean in her, and Jean was a good woman."

"It's not like that."

"Not now, but maybe later, if you play your cards right."

Ian smiled and patted Burt on the shoulder. "I'll look at that engine right after I get back. Don't drive it until I look at it."

Burt sent him off with a wave of his hand. "I know how to take care of my own truck. Now get out of here."

Ian smiled and hopped in his beater truck. It only took two tries to start, and he slowly back out of the driveway and into the street.

Cold Springs was having a brilliant sunny day, not too hot and not too cold considering northern New York was a land of temperature extremes. Today was easy and slow. Just the way he liked it.
He pulled up to Sam's diner and stepped out of his truck. Anxiety hit him hard. Maybe he should have called first. Sam had likely changed her mind about the whole thing. Especially after what her mother had said about him. Not that everything she said wasn't true. He had no business having anything to do with her or messing up her life.

He knocked on the front door.
The little bell above the door rang as Sam opened the door. "Hi."

"Hi, Ian. Come in."

"I didn't know if I should call first. You probably don't—"

"That's fine. I was ready anyway." She grabbed her purse. "Where do you want to go?"

Panic formed a knot in Ian's gut. He hadn't thought this thing through. For an entire year he'd been careful not to draw attention to himself. He'd never intended on going into a public place with her. A restaurant could raise the stakes to dangerous levels. He didn't give two shits what others thought about him, but he didn't want Sam to be humiliated by his doing. There were no pizza delivery places for miles so he'd picked up two frozen pizzas at the grocery store the next town over. If word got around that they were seeing each other, when in fact they clearly were not, the town wouldn't let Sam forget it. Any customers she hoped to gain in this town would be lost.

He swallowed hard, nodded to the brown paper bag he carried. Nothing good ever came from lying. "I was hoping we could eat here. I bought a couple pepperoni pizzas. I thought we could cook them up here. I hope that's okay."

She seemed confused. Or disappointed. But what did it matter? This wasn't a date. Just a payment of gratitude. Nothing more.

"That's…fine," she answered, slipping the handle of her purse over the coat rack. "We certainly have plenty of places to sit."

She strolled into the kitchen and appeared with a bottle of wine. "It isn't fancy."

"I don't drink." His response was automatic. I don't think it's wise with my past, he wanted to add, but didn't.

Sam set the bottle down on the counter. "Oh, um…do you like soda? I have all kinds."

"Whatever's good." He wiped his palms off on his jeans and sat down at one of the tables. "I don't mean to put you out. If you had other plans—"

"No, no plans. Just lots of work left to be done, but I could really use a break."

"What else do you need to do?"

She paused, as if going over a list in her head. "I still have shelves to stock, more cleaning. There's always cleaning, but the majority is done, I suppose."

Just then a kitten appeared around his ankles. He looked down at the delicate orange ball of fur and held his hand out for it to sniff. The cat rubbed its face on his index finger and purred loudly. "So Burt struck, I see."

"He certainly did." Sam approached the table with two large glasses. She took the frozen pizzas and placed them on two pans and disappeared with them into the kitchen. "I'm naming him Chance because he represents my second chance coming here."

"So you're keeping him?"

"Why not? I've never owned a pet."

He chuckled. "I had a German shepherd growing up."

"I remember." Sam laughed. "He and you were inseparable. Did he die of old age?"

"I don't know. Mom got rid of him right after —
" He paused, remembering the letter his mother
had written. Euthanized. She didn't want any
trace of her son around. He had shamed them.
Mom hadn't come out and said that in the letter
but Ian had assumed that was why. He had
probably made his entire family a laughingstock
to this town. Cold Springs offered no
forgiveness, and to think his family had received
any was just fooling himself. That was the last
letter he'd received from any part of his family.
Mom had come to visit him once, and Ian had
refused to see her, then no one had come again.
He knew it must be hard for them, especially
Mom, and he wasn't going to force himself on
any of them. It would be better for everyone to
just forget about him, if possible, and hopefully
they would all find peace in their lives.

Sam was looking at him with a strange
expression on her face. Heat rose at the back of
his neck as embarrassment suddenly got the best
of him. Coming here tonight had been a huge
mistake.
"Things must have been pretty hard on you."

He shrugged, at a loss for words. He didn't
want her pity. He didn't want anything. Just
the damn pizza already.

As if on cue, the oven timer buzzed. Thankful for something to break the tension, Ian went to the kitchen to get the pizza. He came back, set it down on one of the adjoining tables.

When Sam had gathered forks and a spatula, she sat down and held the plates as he served. Her stomach growled, loud enough for him to hear.

"It's funny how sometimes I'm too busy to think about food now." She laughed. "I ate all the time when I was working at the agency. I guess it has something to do with brain work versus physical work."

"You don't look it. Like you ate all the time, I mean."

"Uh, thanks."

He smiled. "I'm sorry, I didn't mean to embarrass you. I just meant a lot of women your age have put on weight. You haven't."

"You know I've always been gangly."

Anything but the sort, Ian thought but kept quiet. He couldn't deny that he was attracted to her. She was cute as a kid, but now. Now she was a knock out, even in work clothes covered with kitchen grease.

"I always figured you were too good for me."

He hadn't meant to say that.

Sam put her slice down. "What?"

"I guess that's why I left you stranded that night. What I mean is, Jane Benton was just a piece of tail. Like I told you, I was a stupid kid back then. I abandoned you for a girl I knew would put out." When she didn't respond, he added, "I would have wanted to, um, do it with you, too, but you…you just weren't that type of girl."

Christ, that sounded like a line. He wanted to say something to fix it but nothing came to mind. Sam looked away, picked up her fork and toyed with the topping of her pizza. Color flushed her cheeks and he didn't know if he'd embarrassed or insulted her. The guy before prison had been a selfish ass. The ex-con wasn't much better. Tonight was a mistake. He should have never come here.

He quickly finished his pizza, stood and cleared his plate. "I got to get going. I have to get an early start tomorrow."

"Oh," she quickly answered, her expression questioning. "Okay."

He quickly washed his own dishes then let himself out without another word.

CHAPTER FIVE

Sam was downstairs before sunrise the next morning. She hurriedly showered, dressed, and unlocked the front door well before seven.

She hadn't slept well. Ian had been on her mind all night. He hadn't stayed after eating only one slice of pizza, claiming he had some estimates to do on a new deck for the Fitzpatricks. Sam tried not to feel slighted. Of course, the man had things to do. He was trying to start up a business. And last night certainly wasn't a date! He was thanking her for her business, just as he had stated. That was all, and he had said she wasn't the type of girl that he'd normally take advantage of, which was sweet and she should have felt flattered over. His admission seemed genuine.

Loneliness hit her hard and fast. Whenever she would feel alone in the city, she would call up Maddy, her co-worker. Maddy could type over a hundred words per minute and party as hard as she worked. Even though Sam wasn't much of a partier, Maddy could always cheer her up.

Sam wondered what Maddy's hair color of the month was now. If it wasn't jet black with wide purple streaks, the whole thing was hot pink or whatever color could call the most attention her way. Maddy was fun and flirty, everything Sam was not. Maddy would frequently tease her about her lack of a social life, but Sam never minded. She enjoyed her lackluster life. It was peaceful and organized, but right now Sam missed Maddy. Maddy would know what to do about Ian. Not that Sam would ever act on any of Maddy's suggestions, but she was an excellent shoulder to cry on. Something Sam really needed right now.

Grabbing her cell phone from the counter, she started to text her then stopped. Five a.m. on a Saturday was not the best time to bother Maddy. The girl was likely hung over from the night before or not home entirely. She'd wait until later.

The bell over the door chimed as Burt walked in. "Mornin'."

"Hi, Burt." Sam started the coffeemaker. Burt had come by for coffee every morning since she'd arrived in Cold Springs. "You're here early."

"I wouldn't miss interview day for the world."

Sam's heart nearly tripped a beat. She'd been so distracted with Ian that she'd almost forgotten about the two interviews she had set up today. She hoped one of them would work out. She wanted to hire only one waitress and one cook. No one had answered her ad for a cook yet. Hopefully someone would soon.

"Ian wasn't home last night around suppertime."

Sam didn't pretend not to presume Burt hadn't known exactly what had transpired last night. She couldn't hide her grin. "What was said about me?"

"Oh, nothing. I just noticed that Ian's truck was parked outside."

"He brought me pizza in appreciation for hiring him."

"Oh?" Burt's expression was ridiculous.

Sam snapped a towel at him. "That's right, 'oh.' One piece of pizza and he didn't even finish his soda and he was gone. Nothing. Happened."

Sam expected more jokes. She didn't expect Burt's expression to turn serious. "Ian's had a hard life. He's seen things that would break most people."

Sam waited for Burt to go on, but he stopped and drank his coffee. Sam busied herself with the diner, turning on the radio and the little television in the upper corner over the counter. She came back to the counter and leaned her elbows across from Burt. "How come you took him under your wing like you did anyway?" Burt didn't make eye contact with her, just looked straight ahead, drinking his coffee. "I don't know what you mean."

"Yes, you do. This whole town treats Ian Woods like scum except you. Why? You didn't even know him before I left for New York."

Burt drank thoughtfully. He set his cup down with a tired sigh. "There are a lot of things you don't know about me."

"Like what?"

"Your aunt was good to me."

"Tell me something I don't know." Sam didn't know what he was getting at, but she had a feeling Burt would stop talking and she didn't want that.

"Jean accepted me for who I was, always had. She knew I had a shady past, had run ins with the law when I was younger and she stood by me anyways." Burt met her stare. "Your mother always said your aunt could do better. I was a bum and I was no good for her, but Jean didn't care. She told your mother to mind her own business."

Burt smiled, as if recalling the memory with fondness and love. "Least I could do was return the favor to someone else. The boy needed a new start. He needed a break, and someone had to give him one. It might as well be me. And he turned out to be a damn fine young man too."

Sam didn't know what to say. She couldn't believe what she'd just heard. No one had ever said a word about Burt ever breaking the law. "What'd you do?"

"Does it matter?"

No, it didn't. She loved Burt, always had. "No, of course not. I just—"

"Then get me another cup of coffee and don't worry about it."

~ * ~

A couple hours passed when the front door opened and a young woman popped her head inside. "Um…hi."

"Hi." Sam and Burt spoke at once.

"I'm here for the waitress interview?" She ended her statement with a question.

The girl was cute to say the least. Her hair was blond, cut off bluntly above the shoulders to reveal large gold earrings swinging from each side of her head like miniature chandeliers. Gorgeous curves, short black skirt, tight in all the right places, an even tighter linen, flowered blouse which exposed a generous portion of cleavage. A pushup bra had to be the only explanation how she got her D-size girls up that high.

Rushing to meet her, Sam extended her hand. "I'm Sam. I own Jean's Diner."

"I'm Chrissy Kramer." Chrissy's handshake was weak and nervous.

"Nice to meet you." Sam pulled out a chair at the nearest table. "Why don't we sit down and talk?"

"I'm Burt" came the voice at the counter.

Chrissy crossed the room to shake his hand. "Hi, Burt. I'm Chrissy."

"Pleased to know ya." Burt beamed from ear to ear.

"Do you own Jean's Diner, too?"

"No, but I knew Jean very well. Where ya from?"

"I just moved here from the city." Chrissy nodded. "I go to college part-time."

"What are you studying?"

"I'm not sure yet."

Burt took a drink of his coffee. "How can you be studying what you're not sure of?"

Chrissy laughed nervously. "I...I guess I don't know."

"I think I'd rethink what you're doin'. Spending an awful lot of money on something you're not sure of doesn't make much sense to me."

Chrissy didn't know what to make of Burt's comment. Sam could see that clearly on her face. Most people didn't know how to take Burt. "Can I get you some coffee?" Sam hoped to ease the poor girl's discomfort. "Soda? Water?"

"Water would be nice."

Sam quickly got her a bottle of water. She placed a reassuring hand on her shoulder as she handed her the bottle.

"Who on earth drinks water this time in the morning?" Burt asked.

"Don't mind him. He's…uh…he's an early customer," Sam explained. She had a feeling she'd be explaining Burt to a lot of people in the very near future.

"Oh, that's okay." Chrissy flashed an infectious smile. "He's a cutie."

Burt grinned from ear to ear.

Sam grabbed her notebook off the counter. "Why don't we sit down and get started?"

Chrissy followed her to the table. "How come your name isn't Jean?"

"Jean was my aunt."

Chrissy nodded. "You should name it Sam's Diner."

Sam smiled. She'd thought briefly about changing the name. Not to Sam's Diner but to something trendy involving coffee, but it seemed to be a disservice to all that Aunt Jean had built up. Everything which Sam hoped to carry on. Without her, Sam would still be in New York. Plus Jean had a reputation here. When the people of Cold Springs came here, they expected a hot beverage and a good meal. And lots of it. Sam had no right taking that away.

"So," she began. "I need to hire a waitress."

"She's hired." Burt strolled over with coffee mug in hand and pulled up a chair. He stared at her cleavage like a dehydrated horse at water. "When can you start?"

"No, Burt. She's not. Not yet anyway."

"Well, she looks promising."

Sam ignored him. "So tell me about your work experience."

Chrissy rested her arms on the table. "I don't have any, but I like people. I like talking to them. I like making sure they're happy. I think everyone should be happy, don't you?"

"I do," Burt agreed.

The bell on the door sounded and a woman suddenly came in. Middle fifties, maybe early sixties, she was close to six feet tall and built like an oak tree. Gray-brown hair was pinned in a sixties era beehive. She wore white scrubs and a white smock, buttoned to the neck. Shoes were something nurses — or waitresses — wore for comfort when working a double shift.

"Hi." Sam stood. "May I help you?"

The woman crossed the room in three easy strides. "Martha Simms. I'm applying for the waitress position."

Chrissy had been the first to response to her newspaper ad. Sam had simply put a phone number, no address or location. "How did you find the address?"

"This is Cold Springs. It wasn't too hard to figure out."

"Martha." Burt crossed his arms in front of his chest. "How's Bill?"

"He's fine, except for the gout again. Can't even walk this time."

"You two know each other?" Sam asked.

"It's Cold Springs," they both said at once.

Sam pulled out another chair. "Okay, well…I was just interviewing. Martha, why don't you join us and I'll interview both of you together?" Sam hadn't planned on a dual interview, and her heart raced with nerves. She'd never interviewed anyone for anything before. Part of her wondered if they would find her a fraud, and soon the whole county would know she had no clue what she was doing. That all of this was new, all very much out of her league, and she would fail. Fall flat on her face and be known to the people of Cold Springs as the niece who had ruined Jean's Diner.

Sam squared her shoulders. "Chrissy, this is Martha. Martha, Chrissy. Chrissy was just telling me about her work experience. Martha, how about you?"

"I have been in the food industry for over twenty-five years."

Burt got himself another cup of coffee and sat down. "Martha was the lunch lady up at the high school for ten of that. Until she told off Henry Kegg."

"He mowed over my rose bushes!" Martha defended. "His wife's the school superintendent. Thinks she can pull her weight around the whole neighborhood. I told them I want to be paid for my rosebushes. They weren't cheap and the Keggs make damn more money than I do."

"They still don't get along," Burt added.

"Everybody running that school thinks they're better than everybody!" Martha slammed her fist on the table, making Sam jump. "And they never paid me for the roses."

Sam wrote down Martha's name. "Where else have you worked?"

"La Trattoria, The Coffee Mug, most recently The Rustic Crab."

"I like to eat," Chrissy piped up. "I like helping people eat."

"You're hired." Burt didn't even hesitate.

"Burt—"

Martha stood. She pulled a business card from her pocket and handed it to Sam. "This is my card with my phone number. When she doesn't work out, call me."

"She'll work out," Burt said. "Martha, give my best to Bill."

"Chrissy's not hired yet." Sam took the card. "No one's hired yet. Martha, please excuse Burt. Burt, you are out of line."

"Why?" Burt looked insulted. "Chrissy can do the job just as good as anybody."

"I can." Chrissy beamed and placed a hand on Burt's.

Sam put her head in her hands and sighed. "All right. You're hired."

"Yay!"

"You're both hired," Sam called as Martha started to leave. "On a trial basis."

"What do you mean?" Chrissy looked confused.

"That means you work and we'll see how you do before we make you permanent." Sam noticed Martha standing by the door frowning. "What do you say, Martha?"

Martha was silent for a long while. Sam wondered if she was guessing that she'd probably be doing all the work while Chrissy served as eye candy for the male customers. Had that been what Sam had done? Oh Lord, she was a horrible boss already! Martha would probably be calling the labor board on her within a month.

"You never discussed the pay," Martha finally spoke.

"Three seventy-five an hour plus tips." Sam had researched what the average wage for a waitress was. New York State said that one didn't have to pay minimum wage as long as waitresses could collect their own tips to equal minimum wage. Sam wondered if that was enough. She didn't see how one could live on waitress wages and she felt more than guilty about it.

Martha nodded toward Chrissy. "I want more than her."

Sam hadn't expected Martha's reaction. "I really—"

"I have more experience."

"Chrissy has more personality," Burt chimed in.

"Thank you, Burt!" Chrissy touched his arm.

"And I can cook." Martha pursed her lips.

"Why don't we see how it goes?" Sam stood. "Can you start Sunday at five a.m.?"

Martha nodded. "That will be fine."

"And Chrissy, I'll start you out afternoon shift. Will that work?"

"I have all morning classes, so that's fine."

"I'll try to be here in the afternoon then." Burt sighed.

~ * ~

Sam woke with the alarm at four a.m. the next morning. Grabbing her clothes, she headed into the bathroom, only to find cold water in the shower. Still in her cotton jammie pants and T-shirt, she hurried down to the basement to check the hot water heater. Not that she knew anything about how to fix it, if that was indeed the problem.

The basement was a scary place. The crooked wooden stairs was enough to easily break an ankle. Stone foundation, crawling with spiders and sounds of dripping water everywhere. Sam had been down here before, but it was not a place she willingly looked forward to visiting. If an ax murderer could hide out anywhere, it would certainly be here. Where was the hot water heater? If she had no hot water heater, how did she once have hot water? She stared at the monstrous boiler that took up much of the space. It was a maze of piping and valves, looking like a villain in a steampunk novel. If hot water came from that thing, she hadn't a clue where to start. One person was sure to know.

She thought about calling someone else. She knew she should call someone else, but Ian was the first she called.

And he came right over. She barely had time to change into jeans and a clean shirt and pull her hair up in a ponytail. She held the flashlight as she followed Ian down the basement steps. "Where's the hot water heater?"
"You don't have one." He inspected the boiler like he had been working around them his whole life. "You don't need one. You have a boiler that makes hot water. This is an indirect-fired hot water heater."

He must have seen her looking at him like he had three heads because he explained, "Your boiler makes your hot water."

"Well, it's not making hot water today, so what's the problem?" Sam's head began to pound. She hadn't meant to snap. Aunt Jean just served meals and coffee. She couldn't have known anything about boilers.

Ian didn't seem the slightest bit affected by her irritation. He pulled the front cover off the boiler and tinkered around with something. "Here you are. The thermocouple's bad."

"The what?"

"Your pilot's out." He removed some kind of probe-like thing. A copper tube stuck out of one end of it. "The pilot won't light, so—never mind. Look, it's twenty bucks and I'll fix it for you."

"That's all?"

Sam hadn't realized she was shining the flashlight in his face until he took it from her. For a brief moment, his hand touched hers. It was calloused but warm.

"On second thought," he said with a wink, "I'll be back for breakfast and we'll call it even."

Sam had bacon, scrambled eggs, and toast ready by the time Ian returned with the new boiler part. He'd had to drive into the city and find a hardware store willing to give him credit for his business. He said it like that was something rare. Sam wondered if Ian had credit problems. Sam had always had excellent credit, and she couldn't imagine having the inconvenience of not getting credit. Good credit had always just been commonplace to her.

He ate at the counter as she poured herself a cup of coffee. "Thank you. Again."

He bit half a slice of toast in half and swallowed it down with a gulp of coffee. "Thanks for breakfast."

"Can I at least pay you for the part?" She felt cheap. Anyone would have charged her more.

He looked down at his plate. "This was probably twenty bucks worth of food."

"Not hardly."

"Okay, pay me for the part then."

Sam gave him the money for the part.   He seemed to be in a foul mood. She wondered if it was because she'd ruined his plans for the day by calling him so early for a boiler repair. That was what he was in business for, she told herself, yet she couldn't help but feel his moodiness was something more.
She wondered if it was true, that he'd killed someone. She didn't understand how someone could break the law, let alone kill anyone, especially someone who was once the school's star football player. She didn't understand how he could be capable of that kind of violence.

He was staring at her. Ice cold eyes. Hard, intense. Dangerous. Sam wondered if he realized that she was judging him, but how could he?
 "Do you ever want to go back and relive high school?"   Where had that question come from?

"No, not really, but you must. You were the popular one."

He chuckled, thoughtfully took a drink of his coffee. "Yeah, once."

"You probably could be again."

"Probably?" He gave a bitter laugh. "There's no turning back from where I came from, sweetheart."

There it was. Prison. Sam wanted to ask about it. She tried to think of what could have driven him to murder, if that was what he'd done, but couldn't. Maybe Mother and Theresa had their stories wrong. How many times had either of them been wrong about rumors? She'd seen it over the years when her mom told everyone that Theresa was pregnant—again. It had only been wishful thinking on Mother's part. She was prone to stretching the truth. She made her living writing fiction, after all. Maybe Ian just wrote bad checks or embezzlement or something. That would certainly be better than murder.

Sam thought of the flyer she'd received in the mail. It had been her first piece of mail delivered to this address. An invitation to her high school reunion, and it was tonight. She'd given no thought to going and had tossed it in the trash. Still, she remembered the date, just like she remembered the dates of all the dances and proms she'd never went to. Just because nerd girl didn't fit in didn't mean she'd forgotten about them.

She squared her shoulders. This was all wrong, the most senseless thing she'd ever done. She cleared her throat and met Ian's hard stare. "Do you have plans tonight?"
He raised an eyebrow.

"Our high school reunion is at Buster's tonight. Would you want to go…with me?" When he didn't answer, she tried to make light of his impending rejection. "It'd be fun. Jock and nerd girl going…together."

"Don't call yourself that."

"It's what I was. Besides, I don't consider being a nerd a bad thing. I made a living off books."

"You liked to read. You weren't a nerd." He frowned. "Don't put yourself down."

"Well, anyway. Forget it. It was just an idea."

"What time?"

She turned around, surprised. "Cocktails start at seven."

"Should I meet you here?"
He could have knocked her over with a feather.
"Yeah, sure."

Ha! She was going to her high school reunion with Ian Woods, captain of the football team…now ex-convict.

Oh my God! What had she just done?

CHAPTER SIX

True to his word, Ian picked her up at the diner promptly at six-thirty. Sam had changed into five different outfits and had decided on a simple black dress with a white lace shawl. Now, glancing out the front window, Sam watched Ian get out of his truck and felt seriously overdressed.

He wore faded blue jeans with a hole in the left knee and a white T-shirt. No jacket. His hair tussled like he just got out of bed. Perfectly dead sexy, yet perfectly inappropriate for a class reunion. At least by New York City's standards. Probably fine for a Cold Springs reunion. Was she overdressed?

She opened the door for him, and he gave a slow whistle. Warmth coiled in the pit of her stomach. Something that had been long since dead opened its eyes and gave a wide, open mouthed yawn. Maybe it had never been dead. Maybe it had never existed until now. Maybe it had just been born. Confidence. Sexy. Sam felt it, maybe for the first time. And she liked it.

"Look at you! I didn't think…we were only going to Buster's, so I didn't dress up."

"Oh, that's all right." Sam suddenly felt uncomfortable, wondering if her expression that easily gave away her thoughts. Buster's wasn't exactly the location one would like a high school reunion to be held. It was a burger and beer joint more than anything, but they always had a really good steak dinner too. Sam supposed in a town as small as Cold Springs with a high school class of less than twenty-five students, Buster's was about as grand as could be expected. It wasn't even in Cold Springs but about fifteen miles away, just a little hole in the wall that everyone always knew about.

Ian was staring at her. His eyes slowly ran the length of her, sending chills up her spine despite the October evening. "You look nice."

"Thanks."

"I mean, really nice."

"Um…thanks."

"That dress must have been expensive."

Sam looked down at herself. It had been. She'd bought it last year to attend a cocktail event for one of her author clients. That seemed so long ago now. Never would she have thought she'd be wearing it to her high school reunion.

"Do you want to go now?"

"Sure," she answered.

He seemed uncomfortable, and taking her lead, followed her to his truck.

"You have to get in on my side." He held the door for her. "The passenger side doesn't work anymore."

"Oh." Sam jumped behind the wheel. Cautiously, she slid to the passenger side, ever mindful of her skirt wanting to catch on the interior fabric and slide up. Ian's gaze was on her legs, she noticed, as heat rose to her cheeks. His expression was focused, dangerous, hot as hell. She quickly slid over to the passenger seat and he got in beside her.
He turned the ignition. Nothing.

"C'mon," he muttered under his breath and tried again. Nothing. "Dammit!"

He got out, popped the hood and did something underneath. He jumped in, turned the key, and the engine roared to life.

"We could have taken my car." Sam should have offered to begin with. It had been her idea to come, after all.

"My truck not good enough for you?"

"No, I—" His sarcasm both shocked and hurt her, and she had nothing to say.

"I'm sorry."

"It's okay."

"No, no it's not. I'm sorry." He gave a long sigh and ran a hand through his hair.

The ride to Buster's was long and silent. Sam tried to make small talk first about weather then about his work, but she was only met with short, clipped responses so she gave up and went silent.

When they pulled into the dirt parking lot, she was surprised to see that it hadn't changed in years. Just a hole in the wall with a bar, occasional live music by some local band, and a limited menu with burgers and fries.

The place was packed. Getting out of the truck, Sam immediately recognized faces she hadn't seen in years. The same insecurities of a teenager came back tenfold. Around these people, she still felt like the same nerd. What else had she expected?

Sam suddenly hated herself. She'd come here just to prove something to herself, and that was pathetic. A level even the teenage Sam would never have stooped to.

"Maybe we should go."

Ian's expression was concerned. "You feeling okay?"

"Fine, but maybe this was a mistake. I was never the popular one—"

"Samantha Stone!"

Sam turned to see Cara Thompson. Cara hadn't changed a bit. She'd been the head cheerleader, still had the perfect curves, and was dressed in tight jeans and a casual sweater.

Sam pulled her shawl tightly around herself. Man, was she overdressed!

"Hi, Cara. How are you?"

Cara caught her in an embrace. "Stone, right? I mean was Stone. You're probably married now."

"Still Stone." Sam hugged her back.

Cara stepped back. "Oh, I'm so sorry. You never married?"

"It's quite all right." Sam shook her head. She knew Cara hadn't meant anything by her comment, yet it still stung. High school in Cold Springs, probably in any small town for that matter, had a way of staying with you. "Cara, you must remember Ian Woods."

Cara smiled, nodded slightly. She took a step back. "Well, I better get inside. Good seeing you, Sam."

Odd. And awkward. She turned to Ian. He didn't seem the slightest bit concerned. "Wanna go in?"

"If you do."

He touched the small of her back.

It happened so suddenly Sam wondered if she'd imagined it. However, his touch lingered there just a few seconds longer, verifying that it was not her imagination. A small act but something so intimate she felt as if he'd taken ownership of her. Strangely not an unpleasant feeling.

They climbed the three wooden steps that led inside the bar. Classic rock blared, making everyone shout their conversations. Sam had never been comfortable in crowds, or in bars, or around loud music, and she cautiously shrunk back against Ian. His body was lean and hard and somehow comforted her.

All too soon, Ian disappeared toward the bar and came back with two sodas. "I didn't get you diet because you don't need it." He grinned.

"Thank you." Sam smiled. She remembered him looking at her can of diet soda the night they'd shared pizza. The fact that he remembered was impressive. She doubted Ian had ever remembered anything about her back in high school.

Various people came up and started conversations with her. Sarah Parker spoke to her for a good half hour. Sam briefly told her about her life in New York City and about opening the diner. She'd brought a few flyers she'd made for the new business and passed those out to everyone who spoke to her. Ian stayed at the bar, not really saying anything to anyone.

Strange, the captain of the football team should be talking to everyone. Nerd girl shouldn't be more outgoing than Ian Woods. But she was and it was weird. He sat at the bar gripping his drink, clearly uncomfortable. Ian was no longer popular in this town, and from the looks people were giving him, he certainly wasn't wanted here.

Sam approached him. His smile was slow, gentle, and it seemed grateful for her presence. She felt a connection grow between them just then. It was unexpected and surprising, and Sam didn't know what to make of it. "I'm ready to call it a night. How about you?"

"Are you sure?"

"Most definitely."

They started to leave when two men blocked their path. The first one was huge, rock solid like a bull in a china shop. "Well, if it isn't book girl and the jock turned murderer."

It was Frank Rogers. Star football player. He and Ian had been inseparable in school.

"You into ex-cons, Sam?" Brad Smith looked her up and down, his gaze landing on her breasts. Frank nudged Ian with the neck of his beer bottle. "You didn't tell her, Woods?"
Ian took Sam's hand and without speaking, pushed by them, all the while pulling Sam with him.
Frank was quick on their heels.

"I never knew you were so into trash, nerd girl." Sam would have stopped, but Ian kept pulling her.
This wasn't high school anymore, but of course a small town like this bred immaturity, especially from people who never had the guts to leave. Why did she even think coming here would be a good idea?

Ian had already made his way to the truck. "Get in." He nearly shoved her inside.

The engine growled to life on the first try, and they didn't say a word to each other the entire way home. She couldn't help but wonder what it was like for him to be on the other end of the popularity spectrum, to start life in the perfect clique of people and then in the blink of an eye have friends and family hate you. Sam had often felt misunderstood by many but never despised.

He pulled into his secluded driveway, threw the truck in park and slammed the wheel with both fists, making her jump.

"I'm sorry." He gave a long sigh. "Do you want to come in for a drink?"

Sam hadn't expected this. She knew she should refuse, but she was curious. She wondered where he lived. Well, she knew where, but she had no idea how he lived. Neat freak or slob? Cat or dog? Pictures of children?

She had no idea if he had children.

"Have you ever had kids?"

"Excuse me?"

"I asked you if you have any children."

"None that I'm aware of."

Sam didn't know why she felt relieved.
Children were something Sam never considered
in her life. Perhaps someday, should she meet
the right person, but someday seemed so far off,
so why even think about it? Besides, she was
always too busy. Now she was busier than ever
before.

So he had no baggage. Well...unless you
counted prison.
Sam saw a light on in the ranch-style house on
the property and could make out the form of
Burt slumped over in one of the reclining chairs
with a book open across his chest and the
television playing across from him.

"I live out here." Ian pulled his keys from the
ignition and hopped out.
A flight of stairs led to the second story of the
garage. There was a small wooden deck in the
front which wrapped around the side. Flower
boxes had been constructed along the top railing
and contained bright orange marigolds, still
untouched by frost.

Sam followed him to the side of the garage and up the stairs to the little apartment above. Ian slid a key in the door and switched on the light. He held the door for her to enter first. "Burt rents the place to me pretty cheap. I figure I'll rent from him at least until I get back on my feet then find a real place so Burt can rent this out to someone who will pay him more."

"I'm sure he wouldn't allow you to pay more if you wanted to," Sam said, knowing how highly Burt regarded Ian.

"I tried, believe me, but he wouldn't hear of it."

"I can imagine."

Sam glanced around the place. It was a simple, one-room apartment with a door leading off to a small bathroom. His furniture was sparse, some looking secondhand and nothing matching, but it was cozy and comfortable, just the same. Ian grabbed two sodas from the refrigerator and handed one to her.

"Thanks."

Gesturing toward the sofa, he sat down. Sam sat at the other end. A kitten immediately greeted her by walking across her lap and settling in. He was the same orange color as Chance. "I see you couldn't resist either."

"Burt feeds every stray in the neighborhood then wonders why he's overrun with kittens."

The kitten batted her hands. Sam smiled, the stress of the evening gradually fading. Silence slowly filled the room. The evening was exceptionally warm for fall. Ian had left the door open, and frogs from the nearby pond sung in the distance. It was nice and lulling, definitely relaxing and something she needed after the shambles that the night turned out to be.

"I supposed you heard everything about my past tonight."

She was surprised to hear him talk about it. "It's none of my business."

He took a long swig of soda. He hadn't drunk alcohol. Some people never drank for various reasons, but Sam couldn't help but wonder if Ian had a problem with it. "No, I think I should tell you. You gave me a chance hiring me after your mother warned you about me. Not many people would have done that, and I appreciate it."

"I needed cheap labor." She tried to make light of the situation, but Ian wasn't laughing.

"Still, you didn't have to do it."

He was silent for a long while. Maybe he had changed his mind about telling her. It didn't matter. Ian had his demons. Sam surmised he had a lot of them, and it simply was what it was, but it was definitely not her business. She didn't feel in danger around him, and as long as he was not a threat, what was in his past didn't matter.

"You know I have a sister, Roxanne." He finally spoke.

Sam recalled a dark-haired girl from school. "She's younger than you."

Ian nodded. "By three years."

"Mike, her boyfriend, beat her pretty bad. Knocked her up, even hit her while she was pregnant. She lost the kid but got pregnant again. She had this one, a little boy. They call him Theodore...Teddy. God, he'll be a teenager pretty soon."

"You haven't gone to see him?"

Ian glanced at Sam. Blue eyes full of uncertainty. That uncertainty made him suddenly appear younger and vulnerable. Gone was the arrogant confidence of years past.

He shook his head. "I'd be the last person Roxy would want to see. Anyway, I had gone over to Roxy's place. She was living with Mike in a trailer park. A real dump, but what else could you expect from that scumbag? I was in the back room at the time. Mike didn't know I was there. He was drunk again and started in on my sister, beating on her. Mike started shoving her around, and I came out and hit him. I'd listened to Roxy brag this guy up for over six years. I'd seen the bruises, seen the way she'd lie to our parents about how she got them. It was ridiculous."

Sam watched as Ian's expression changed from one of hurt to sheer anger.

"Mike fell like a ton of bricks. I guess he had an aneurism explode in his brain or something. That's what I was later told. The punch I threw wouldn't have killed a normal person. Anyway, I went up for ten years on manslaughter charges but got parole for good behavior."

"Couldn't the police have listened to your side of things? You were defending your sister."

"They tried to get second-degree murder because they said I'd intended to hurt him. I had, just didn't intend on killing him." Ian's expression suddenly masked to somewhere very far away. The hands that he'd balled up into fists began trembling.

Sam reached for his hand and squeezed it. "Thank you."

"For what?"

"For telling me what happened. I'm sorry."

He pulled away and quickly stood. His expression turned hard, cold, turned to someone she didn't know. "I don't need pity."

"I wasn't—" She hadn't meant to insult him. She stood, set her soda can on the kitchen counter. "I'd better go."

"I'll take you home."

"It's not far. I can walk."

Sam couldn't have expected the next moment. They were standing too close, and they bumped into each other. She looked at him, and he looked down at her. The evening had been too stressful. She should just back away, but she didn't realize what he was doing until it was too late.

He bent toward her, and she stood up on her toes. His hand cradled her jaw, his calloused thumb gently brushing over her lips. The kiss was innocent enough, his lips barely brushing over hers. Her heart tripped and beat nearly out of her chest. She laid her palm on his cheek, feeling the stubble of his beard.

Ian broke the kiss and stepped back. "I'm sorry."

"It's okay."

"You say that all the time."

"No, really—" She didn't know what else to say. She wondered about Ian's life, wondered how many other times before he'd had to deal with rude comments and gossip about his past. Would he stay in Cold Springs?

The thought surprised her, but she really couldn't imagine him being able to put up with small town minds and gossip for long. No one ever really was supposed to care what others thought of them, but how could one not? Especially when you were trying to build a new life. Starting over would be so much easier in a town that didn't share his past.

Sam didn't want him to go. They were both a part of Cold Springs, and they could get through it together. Couldn't they? The thought both surprised and scared her. Sam had never thought about the two of them together, as a team. It fit. It didn't make sense most of the time, but it fit.

Ian gently rested a hand on her shoulder. "C'mon. I'll take you home."

CHAPTER SEVEN

Sam was a bundle of nerves. She told herself it was because tomorrow was opening day and today the health inspector was coming. It had nothing to do with what happened with Ian Woods last night.

Ian had kissed her, and her knees had gone weak. She had no right feeling anything toward him. He was an ex-convict who had murdered someone.

Murdered someone who had been harming his family. His crime didn't seem as bad as everyone made it out to be. Everyone talked about how horrid he was, like he was this uncontrollable raging monster. They didn't talk about how he was protecting his sister. No one spoke of how he was trying to defend her.

She drummed her fingers on the counter and tried to calm herself with deep breathing. If this inspection did not go well, she was finished.

"Are you going to just stand there or do I get a cup of coffee?"

Absentmindedly, Sam poured Burt his coffee.

"Ian used to be a lot more fun before he went to jail. Now he's just a mess."

Sam looked at him. Burt's expression told her that he had ulterior motives. "Why are you telling me this?"

"I fixed his place up pretty nice, huh?"

Sam laughed. "You don't miss a trick, do you?"

"Not really. All I'm saying is he has his problems. Life won't be easy with him, but he's loyal. He'll stick by you."

"I'm not marrying him."

"Not now, but you never know." Sam didn't miss the look of longing in Burt's expression. No doubt from missing Aunt Jean. She and Burt had been inseparable. Though they lived separately, they spent most days together.

She handed him one of the new menus. "I had these redone. What do you think?"

Burt reviewed it like he was reading War and Peace. After about thirty minutes, he blurted, "Where's the eggs Benedict?"

"I took it out."

"And the sausage gravy over biscuits?"

"Gone."

"Why?"

"I wanted to keep things simple. At least for now."
Burt pierced her with a critical glare. "Ian can cook, you know. He's working every odd job he can find and none of it's steady. You could hire him."

"No."

"Why not?"

"Because…" Why not was a good question. Maybe…

Chrissy burst through the door. "Good morning, everyone!"

"Good morning, Chrissy." Sam stepped toward her. She had asked Chrissy to start today, as a practice run to show her the ropes. She had a feeling Martha wouldn't need any practice. "Welcome to your first day."

"I'm really excited."

"You look nice today, Chrissy." Burt spun around in his seat.

Sam motioned her behind the counter. "I'll show you where everything is and where you can put your purse. I have the inspector due here any minute."

Sam had no more than shown Chrissy around when as if on cue, a tiny man came through the door that Chrissy had failed to shut. He was dressed in a navy blue workman's uniform with the name "Tom" embroidered on the lapel.

Sam approached him. "Hello, I'm Samantha Stone."

He pulled a clipboard from the briefcase that he carried and took her outstretched hand. "Tom Long, Jefferson County health inspector."

"Nice to meet you. Well...this is the diner."

"And the kitchen is...?"

"Back here." She headed to the kitchen, the inspector following.

"Nervous?"

"A little." She laughed. "Tomorrow's opening day. This is my first attempt at running a business."

Immediately, Sam regretted her big mouth. Now he would know she was a fraud. So stupid!
"You know about New York State's point system, correct?"

"I don't."

The inspector sighed. "New York has a point system. Zero to thirteen is an A. Fourteen to twenty-five is a B, and twenty-eight or higher is a C."

"C is bad?"

He looked at her as if she'd sprouted horns. "C is bad."

Sam watched as he ran two fingers across the counter and wrote something down on his clip-boarded papers.

"Is something wrong?"

"This is a 5C." He pointed to the wooden cutting board on the counter.

"A what?"

"Contact with a surface area with unwashed material."

"Well…" No, this was not happening. "What if I throw it out?"

"See that you do."

He went to the cooler and took a thermometer out from his shirt pocket. He set it in the cooler, waited, then took it out and examined it. "Your temperature is off one degree. You need to have this forty-one degrees or below." More writing on the clipboard.

Sam felt like she was going to throw up. "Will I still be able to open tomorrow?"

"Yes, but you'll need to get that fixed right away."

Sam breathed a sigh of relief. Maybe she'd get through this with no problems.

She wouldn't have guessed what happened next would've occurred in a million years. What could have been the largest rat she'd ever seen scurried across the kitchen directly in front of the inspector. Chance scurried after it, catching it in his mouth.

"Oh my God!" The inspector jumped three feet.

Sam caught Chance in her arms, and with the rat still in the kitten's mouth, threw them both out the back door.

"I'm so sorry." She had no idea how the cat had gotten in. She'd purposely double checked and made sure Chance was securely shut upstairs in the apartment. She'd been so certain she had shut the apartment door…at least she thought she had. Maybe because she was so hurried and stressed today she had forgotten.

The inspector was writing so fast, he could run out of ink in no time. "This is a 4K violation. Condition five is rat infestation. Condition four zero is live animals in an establishment. You, madam, will not be opening tomorrow."

Sam couldn't believe what was happening. "Isn't there some way around this?"

"How about money?" Burt was standing behind him. He held a handful of bills. "Two thousand should keep your trap shut."

The inspector stared. Sam stared. Chrissy was frozen like a statue.

"Burt, no." A 5C, a 4K rat infestation violation, now Burt was bribing the inspector. What next? A night in jail?

The inspector snatched the money from Burt's hand, filled out another form and handed it over to her. "Best of luck on your opening day tomorrow."

And with that he packed up his briefcase and left.

Chrissy sat down at the counter. "That was so wrong. He just took the money. It was like something out of a movie."

"Burt, I can't let you bribe… Who walks around with two thousand dollars in their pocket? Who does that?"

Burt just grinned.

"No, really. In New York they'd kill you for that."

"This ain't New York."

"Burt, I can't let you do this."

"It's already done."

Sam didn't know what to say. "I'll pay you back."

"You open tomorrow, right?"

Sam got Burt another cup of coffee. "Right."

"You hire Ian as your cook, and put Jean's eggs Benedict and sausage gravy back on the menu, and we're even."

~ * ~

Sam spent the remainder of the day preparing for tomorrow's opening day. She let Chrissy go home after explaining the ropes for tomorrow to her. She was just about to head upstairs and nuke a frozen dinner when Ian Woods knocked on her door.

She held the door for him. "Hi."
"Hi."

He stood in the diner like a giant towering over her. His clothes were covered with white paint, and his jeans were torn. "I came over to talk to you about what happened last night."

His voice was soft, rugged, and one hundred percent sexy.
"There's no need. Your past is not my concern."

"No, I wanted to tell you. And I wanted to thank you for listening. It feels good, you know? To let it out, especially to someone I trust."

"You trust me?" Warmth coiled in the pit of her stomach. She'd never really given trust much thought, but coming from Ian Woods, after everything he'd been through, trust from him was certainly something rare and she felt honored that he gave it to her.

He was standing too close, and she had the incredible urge to wrap her arms around his neck and kiss him until he was dizzy. Heat rose to her cheeks as they stood there staring at each other. This was all too much, too intense, and she wasn't ready for any of it.

"Would you like a job?" she blurted. "I mean, to work with me, for me. Here. I need a cook, and Burt says you can cook." It wasn't a lie. Martha had called her and informed her that she had thought things over and wouldn't work the same shift as Chrissy. Which meant that Sam would need another cook since no one had ever answered her ad for a full time one.

Ian smiled. He didn't answer right away but was silent for so long she expected him to say no. "I learned to cook in prison."

She didn't know if he expected a response from her. "If you don't take the job, I'll owe Burt two thousand dollars."

"Why?"

"It's a long story," she answered.

"Well, we wouldn't want to be beholden to Burt." Ian flashed her an infectious smile. "I can start tomorrow. Do you want to have dinner with me tonight? I was going to grill burgers, nothing fancy."

This wasn't a good idea. Everything in her told her to decline. She had no business spending any more time with him than necessary. He was bad news, and now he was her employee.

No, that first part wasn't true. He wasn't bad news. He was a friend who had an unfortunate thing happen to him, and he had been defending his family. However, now they had an employer employee relationship.

"Sounds good." She headed toward the stairs. "I'll get my jacket."

~ * ~

Ian couldn't believe Sam was coming over to his apartment again, any more than he could believe she'd offered him a job. He could certainly squeeze in the odd jobs he was working around the diner's hours. He didn't anticipate his construction business being a going concern for some time.

Things were looking up. Things were also getting complicated. He shouldn't have asked Sam to dinner, and now as she rode in the passenger seat of his truck, the reality of things were sinking in. He'd told her that he trusted her. And he did. Trust was something that prison had taught him to never give away.

He could fall for her very easily.

The thought shocked him. He didn't need this complication in his life. He remembered everything his P.O. had said upon his release from prison. Keep your nose clean. Don't get involved. With anything or anybody. Stay a loner. Keep close to family but stay away from romantic relationships, and you'll have a better chance of making it on the outside.

What bad could come from Sam? She was gentle, kind, so different from the life he'd known behind bars. He didn't deserve someone like her in his life, and the last thing he wanted was to cause her any trouble. Ian had no idea where these feelings of protection were coming from. When had he started caring for her? How could it had happened so fast?

He could also be bad for her business. He could drive customers away. Maybe if he stayed in the kitchen when customers were there, and he could walk to work to avoid others seeing and recognizing his truck. Bottom line was he was bad for Sam and bad for her business.

But he needed the money, and he couldn't say no to her. She needed him, and no one had needed him in a very long time. He would just have to be very careful.

When they reached his apartment, he pulled his key from the ignition, hopped out, and held the door as Sam slid across the seat. He picked up the bag of groceries from the truck box. "I won't be able to work full time."

"Oh, I understand. Sometimes is better than nothing, right?"

He didn't answer. Every time he looked at her, he felt like the same kid who knew her in high school. Life was so innocent then. Played out so differently than what he had planned. He hated that arrogant kid he was before prison. That Ian had taken everything for granted, was too cocky for his own good. He wondered if he had never gone to prison if he would use the familiar cheesy pickup lines on Sam, possibly just use her for a one-night stand as was so common of the arrogant kid he used to be. The thought sickened him. Sam deserved better.

He had no business working for Sam or making her dinner. She was too good for him. And if someone saw them together romantically, her business would be ruined.

They climbed the stairs to the deck where he sat down the bag of groceries. His grill was a simple charcoal portable that he'd picked up at a yard sale for five dollars. Nothing fancy, but it cooked a nice burger.

After unlocking the door, he grabbed the seasonings for the burgers and some plates. He noticed Sam stayed outside on the deck. He wondered if it was because of the kiss. Had she liked it?

"Do you see your family?" she asked when he was back on the deck.

Okay. He hadn't expected that.

"No."

"Don't they come over?"

This wasn't something he wished to discuss, but he didn't want to be rude to his future employer either. "They want nothing to do with me."

"But you defended your sister."

He shrugged, reliving the memory of his mother throwing him out the day he'd been released. "My father died while I was still in jail, but he refused to come see me. My mother felt the same. They said I'd made my bed and so lie in it." He flipped the burgers with a long spatula. "They were tired of hearing what the townsfolk around here said to them. So they sold the house and moved to Watertown. They thought being in the city would make them less of a spectacle."

Ian didn't blame them for that. Cold Springs was hardly a town where people minded their own business enough not to judge. The only reason he'd come back to Cold Springs was because of Burt. Burt had convinced him that he belonged here, where'd he'd always lived, and Burt had been the only one to help him out. Ian's past was what it was. There was no changing people, so the only thing he could do was try to change how he felt about what others thought of him. And right now the only person whose opinion mattered was Sam.

The thought surprised him, scared him. He had no right to feel anything toward her. However, in the past few days what she thought of him mattered a great deal. It shouldn't, but it did.

The burgers done, he flipped them onto a plate and took them inside where he set them on the counter. They each dished up a plate and sat on the sofa.

"I can't believe Burt was actually carrying two thousand dollars cash in his wallet." Sam took a bite of her burger, ketchup squirting out the side of her mouth. It was cute and adorable, and he fought the urge to lean over and wipe it away. Or lick it off with his tongue.

The thought made him hard almost immediately. He couldn't recall his last sexual encounter. Before incarceration, sex had always been a physical release. Emotions never had to be factored in. However, spending so much time locked up did something to a person. Made him want things, permanent things like respect, understanding, and companionship with a woman. A woman like Sam.

He watched her wipe the ketchup off her face with a paper towel.

"Burt gets a good pension from the phone company. Trouble is, he spends it as soon as the check comes."

"On what?"

"He goes out to eat nearly every meal."

"He can't be spending all of it. Otherwise he wouldn't have had two thousand dollars in his wallet."

"True."

Ian chuckled.

It was the first time he'd laughed in ten years. And it felt good.

CHAPTER EIGHT

The morning rush was busier than Sam had hoped and showed no sign of slowing well after noon. If not for Martha and Ian, Sam didn't know how she would have gotten through it. Everyone wanted something all the time, and Sam's feet had never ached so much in her life. She had decided to stay open from the hours of five a.m. to three in the afternoon. Burt had complained because he wanted it open for dinner too, but then again complaining seemed to make Burt happy, regardless.

Chrissy arrived at one just as Martha was leaving her shift. She wandered aimlessly around the dining room saying hi to the people she knew and introducing herself to the ones she did not. A couple of customers had asked her if she was the new owner. She giggled and explained that she couldn't run a restaurant because she was going to college and wasn't sure what she wanted to do when she graduated. She went on about how she liked being a waitress, but it wasn't something she wanted to do for the rest of her life.

The men loved her.

"Sam!" Ian called from the kitchen.

Sam hurried in to see what he wanted. He had at least a dozen burgers going on the grill. He was someone who definitely knew his way around a kitchen.

"I can't read this one." He pointed his spatula to the handwritten order hanging in front of him. Sam plucked it down and studied it, making out nothing. This was the fourth one today.
She hurried to the dining room and called Chrissy over.

Chrissy was all smiles. "Hi, Sam."
"Here's another one. What does this say?"
Chrissy took the slip, studied it and laughed. "I don't know. I can't make out my own writing. I'll go ask again. Sorry."
"Try to remember to take time to write legibly the first time. It saves customers time which is especially important if they're in a hurry. Okay?"

"Okay."

Sam was wiping down the counter when her mother came in. A rush of warmth filled her, which was immediately followed by guilt. Sam never expected Mother to support her efforts on opening day.

Mother sat at the counter, where Sam had a cup of coffee waiting for her. "Hi, Mom. Thanks for coming."

"I need to talk to you immediately, young lady!"

"What's wrong?" Use of the term young lady was always serious and usually had something to do with Theresa.

Mother leaned over the counter, speaking in the loudest whisper she'd ever heard. "Like you don't know! I heard about you and Ian Woods. It's all over town!"

"What is?"

"That you went to your high school reunion with him. Tonya Perkins heard it from Mary Atkins. How can you be so foolish?"

"Mom, I have no idea who those people are."

"Everyone's talking. Doesn't that bother you?"

"Not really. Talk is a good thing. Maybe it will bring more customers in."

Mother looked like she was going to explode. Without even taking a sip of her coffee, she stood up and silently left.

"Mom!" Sam called after her. "Mom, please stay and finish your coffee."

Her mother brushed her off with a wave of her hand.

Sam sighed.

Not half an hour passed before Theresa came in. Irritation hit Sam fast and hard. For once, she'd like to have a disagreement with her mother without her sister butting her nose in.

Sam put on her best fake smile.

"Hello, lovely sister. Would you like to hear about our specials?"

"Don't play games with me, Sam." Theresa took Sam by the arm and pulled her over by the coat rack. "Mom's in tears. I hope you're happy."

"Actually, no. I'm not happy." Sam pulled out of Theresa's grip. "I thought she'd come here to support me on my opening day. I had hoped that both she and you would be here because you were happy for me."

"How can you do this to Mom?"

Sam turned and headed to the kitchen. "I don't have time for this."

She made it into the storage room before bursting into tears.

~ * ~

Ian heard the sound coming from the storeroom. His first thought was that Chrissy was crying about something incidental once again, and he chose to ignore it, but then he saw Chrissy walk into the kitchen and the sound persisted. Setting down the spatula and turning the grill down, he went to investigate. Sam was perched on a stack of tomato sauce cans, her shoulder sagging with each breath. Instinctively, he put his hands on her shoulders. She tensed then relaxed as soon as she realized who it was.

He squatted down beside her. "What's going on?"

"Nothing." She frantically rubbed her eyes with the back of her hand. She started to stand but Ian caught her in an embrace and pulled her down into his lap. It happened too fast, too naturally, as if he'd been holding her so intimately for a lifetime.

"What's wrong?" He gently rubbed her back.

"Nothing. Everything. My mother. She's just…and Theresa."

"It'll get better."

"It's always been like this." She shook her head. "Now just…being here. I have to deal with it more often."

"Me being here isn't helping, honey." It was the first time he'd ever called her by any term of endearment. He hadn't meant to. It had just slipped out, but he liked how it had sounded. "You being here has nothing to do with it."

"Yes, it does. I heard your mother talking, remember?"

She didn't answer and he didn't know what else to say. He should quit and run like hell out of her life as fast as possible. It would be the best thing for her. He certainly wasn't doing her any favors by staying.

He pulled her close and hugged her again. "I better get back to work."

~ * ~

By day's end, Sam didn't think her feet had ever hurt more. Not just her feet, every part of her body ached. To think that she used to spend her days in stilettos now just seemed ridiculous and…just so long ago.

Chrissy had been the first to leave because she had a class to catch. Burt had stayed all morning, loudly explaining to her which customers would be the "good ones," meaning who tipped well and which were the ones who deserved eggshells dumped in their breakfast. Burt had set up a fixed time every Wednesday to meet the guys here to discuss the important gossip of the day as well as pensions, baseball games, and of course, Chrissy. Chrissy attracted more men that Sam had ever witnessed. Problem was, they were all over sixty-five and dirty old men who only bought coffee.

Martha opened tomorrow and for that Sam was thankful. Martha knew her way around the kitchen and ran the place like a tightly run ship, and Sam felt totally inadequate next to her. Someone like Martha should be the one to inherit a diner, certainly not Sam. Sam had a feeling she'd have a better organized day than today at least.

Ian emerged from the kitchen. His T-shirt was drenched in sweat and sticking to him like a second skin. Sam had never had a thing for guys who needed showers, but Ian was incredibly sexy right now, and if anyone was interested in him showering, it was her. With him.

An embarrassing thought. Lord Almighty, what would Mother and Theresa think?

"Thanks for everything you did today." She coughed. "I couldn't have done it without you."

"No problem."

"You're really organized in the kitchen."

"Had to be. We fed hundreds of inmates."

Sam couldn't get used to his offhanded use of the word inmate. Prison life was just same ol' for Ian. Of course, when you spent ten years there, it would be. But how could it be? She didn't like thinking of Ian in a place like that. He deserved better. He deserved a better life and to not have others gossiping about him all the time.

"What are your plans for the rest of the day?" she asked him. It was nearly two o'clock.

"I got a deck to fix. Matt Goings called me last night and asked for me to stop over and give him an estimate." He poured himself a cup of coffee. "How about you?"

"I'm going to clean up here then check stock. I have a feeling we used more supplies today than I expected."

"That's good, right? You packed the place this morning."

"Definitely." She smiled. She hadn't expected to have such a turn out on opening day. It filled her with an unfamiliar sense of pride and accomplishment. Aunt Jean would definitely be proud and happy to see her diner successful again.

The air between them suddenly became charged. All day they'd made small talk, as if tripping over an elephant in the room. Sam wondered if not for Ian's imprisonment if he would be in her life at all. She wondered when the last time he'd been with a woman had been. The thought both surprised and shocked her. She hadn't been with anyone in a very, very long time.

Things between her and Chet had not been platonic, but she couldn't recall the last time they'd been intimate either. It didn't matter. Chet hadn't seen a future with her, and in the end, it had simply made her feel used. She had no intention of doing that again. Even if she had to live the life of a nun. It was better than being disappointed from expectations that had never been there the whole time.

"Did you ever get, um…attacked in prison?"

His look was one of sheer surprise. He raised one eyebrow, and Sam knew that he knew exactly what she was talking about. She shouldn't have asked. "Not in the way you think."

"I'm, uh…sorry."

"It happens, but I got tough fast. You learn to keep your head down, do your work, and if anyone tries to mess with you, you mess them up first. The answer is no."

With that, he plucked his baseball cap off the coat rack and stormed out.

~ * ~

Hours passed and Ian was still pissed. He'd made an ass of himself in front of Sam today. She'd asked if anyone had raped him in prison and he'd simply answered then walked out. His leaving so abruptly probably made her think he was lying. He wasn't, but he could have gotten raped very easily.

It happened to everybody when they first got jailed. Lines were drawn and the weak were a target. Three guys had cornered him his first day. If he hadn't been so young, he wouldn't have been fast enough. They'd all been armed. A toothbrush whittled down to a plastic spike, a simple eating utensil fashioned into a shiv. They'd rushed him all at once, demanding that he was their bitch now.

Ian had played along at first, taking them off guard and when the big one was adjusting his pants, he'd struck. Ian grabbed the shiv, running it into his leg. The one ran off, and the other one rushed him. Ian had ducked then sucker punched him directly in the throat. He'd gone down like a ton of bricks.

They had respected him after that. Sure, there had been a few fights but they had all been self-defense and no one had ever tried cornering him again.

It had also made him wary, always looking back, and never trusting. Sam made him want to trust again. She made him ache for a normal life with no nightmares. She made him hope again.

He was working on splitting the rest of Burt's firewood, the physical exertion gradually draining his anger. He was putting another chunk on the chopping block when he saw a familiar truck pulled into the driveway.

It was Gary Whitmore. Ian hadn't known him long but had taken to him right away. He was a good shit, as Burt had confirmed, and he didn't judge. He just listened like any good shit would do.

"Hey, man." Gary held out his hand and Ian shook it.

"What's happening?"

"Nothing much. Just got off work and seen you out here. Need a hand?"

"Nah," Ian was quick to answer. "I'm just about finished."

"Well, I timed it good." Gary laughed. He offered Ian a cigarette but Ian refused. It took all his strength to say no.

"Crazy weather we been having."

Ian stared at him. Yesterday had been unusually warm and today the wind was stiff and cold. He had a feeling Gary hadn't come here to talk about the weather. Small talk wasn't his forte.

"Have you talked to Roxy lately?"

Gary's question took him by surprise. What Gary had to do with Roxy he had no idea. Truth was, he hadn't contacted her at all despite the advice of his P.O. "No," he simply answered.

"She's a nice girl. Got a good boy, too."

"What are you getting at?" Irritation crept up the back of his neck, giving him an immediate headache.

"Roxy and I have been talking. Truth is, I'd like to start seeing her, but I wanted to tell you first."

"Tell or ask?"

Gary laughed nervously. "Both, I guess. I really care about her and I didn't think it was right not to tell you."

"I appreciate that." Ian did, but it also had nothing to do with him. Roxy didn't want him in her life. Why would she? He'd killed the father of her child.

Gary's visit drove that home tenfold. Real men spoke to their families. If he had any backbone at all, he would have gone to Roxy right after being released and manned up to her. But he hadn't. Instead, he'd buried his head in the sand and ignored the problem like a coward.

He was a coward now.

Ian met Gary's gaze. "You're a good man, Gary. I'm sure you'll make Roxy very happy."

Relief washed over Gary's expression. "Thanks."

Ian clapped him on the shoulder. Truth was, Gary would make a good companion for Roxy and a good father figure for Teddy. He had two little girls from a previous marriage, and as far as he could see, Gary treated them like gold. Ian's irritation gradually sunk to a dull heaviness as Gary continued to make small talk. His P.O. told him to stay away from "what could have been" thoughts. Looking back did no good. But today…how could he not? Not only was he missing out on his sister's life, but he'd missed seeing her little boy, his only nephew, grow up. Ian wanted to do something about it. He wanted to change things, but what if he made things worse? He had already ruined things when he'd tried to protect Roxy before, and look where that had gotten him.

~ * ~

The days passed in a blur. Sam couldn't remember being this busy ever. Work being an agent was always busy, and she was never caught up, but this was a different sort of busy. She hit the ground running upon waking and didn't stop until well after sundown. Every day was something different and the greatest, most surprising part was that she loved it. Self-employment gave her an indescribable satisfaction that working the daily nine-to-five never had.

The breakfast rush left and an unexpected lull came around eleven. Sam took advantage of the time to mop the mud brought in on everyone's feet with the heavy rain that morning. She had just finished when another customer came in. Only he wasn't another customer.
Six-foot-two, tan khakis, and a mint green polo shirt. Chet Tyler. Here. In Cold Springs. Standing in the middle of Jean's Diner.
"Chet."
"Hi, Sam."
"What are you doing here?"

Chrissy had gone out back to smoke again, so Sam took a menu to Chet.
His smile was confident, full of authority. "I wanted to see the place. And you. How have you been?"

"Fine."

He caught her in a hug. It was strong, powerful. Awkward. He wanted to see her? Why? "Just friends" wouldn't warrant a trip all the way up here.

Sam wondered how she would be five years from now. If she had stayed at her job in New York, she would be looking at six weeks of vacation this year. Not that she ever took any, anyway, but the firm always let her sell it back which helped, especially at holiday time. It was like an extra Christmas bonus.
"Coffee?"

"Sounds great." He flashed her a flawless smile.

Sam went around the counter. By the time she had poured Chet's coffee, Chrissy was back from her break. She nudged Sam.

"Who's that?" Her breath was dank with smoke.
Before Sam had time to respond, Chrissy had grabbed the cup and was practically running toward Chet.
"Why'd you let her go after him?"
Sam turned to see Mother coming toward her. She found a seat at the empty counter and sat down. Sam got her a cup of coffee. "Hi, Mom."
"Chet Tyler's come here for you."

Sam nearly choked on her coffee. Mother had met Chet once when she'd brought him home for a brief weekend visit. She'd spent more time with Aunt Jean than Mother, but Mother was all wrapped up in Theresa, so Sam didn't think she'd even notice her absence.

"I have enough on my plate without getting a love life. What about you?" She passed her mother a menu. "You're not seeing anyone."

Mother looked as if Sam had slapped her. "I'm twice his age. And I don't need my daughter's left overs."

"I hear cougars are the new thing. You should get out. It's not healthy being cooped up alone all the time." Sam tried to joke, but the tension was beyond bearable. What did Chet want?

Mother rummaged through her purse and pulled out her wallet. "I've got to go. I have a full schedule today."

"Writing?"

"Yes, writing. Sam, I would think from your years of being an agent that you would know the kind of hard work it takes being an author." She placed a five dollar bill on the counter.

"It's on the house. I realize you work hard, Mom." Sam felt a stab of guilt. She tried to pretend her words didn't hurt, but Sam had obviously hurt Mother as well, judging by her defensive tone. "Writing isn't easy, and you've managed to make a living out of it. That's huge."

"Thank you."

"Why don't you come over tonight for dinner? Just the two of us."

"I'd like that." Sam was surprised and warmed by her offer. Rare was a time when Mother made any effort to spend time alone with her. Not when she had Super Daughter Theresa available 24/7.

Mother left and Sam watched from the window as she hopped into her car parked by the sidewalk. She turned and ran smack into Chet Tyler.

"Oh!"

"Sam." He flashed her a grin with flawless teeth. "I'd like to talk with you tonight. It's important. Call my cell. I'm staying in town."

Sam nodded, suddenly feeling very awkward. She noticed he was holding his wallet and she punched in his bill on the register. "Seven fifty-nine."

He handed her a twenty. "Keep the change. And call me."

Ian was staring at her from the kitchen. He had a strange look on this face, and she wondered if he'd heard her conversation with Chet. "The cooler's fixed."

"Thank you. What do I owe you?"

"Don't worry about it." He wiped his brow with the back of his hand. "I'm your employee, remember?"

She grabbed a rag from the bucket of bleach water she kept on hand and wiped off the counter. "Thank you."

"So…are you going?"

So he had been listening. Jealous much? But why should he be? Sam was merely a friend to Ian. The kisses had been a mistake, and now that she was his employer there would be no future relationship other than a business arrangement.

When she didn't answer, he added, "He looks like those jocks you hated at the reunion."

"He's not that bad." Sam didn't know why she was so quick to come to Chet's defense. Maybe she resented Ian's judgement.

"Do what you want, but don't say I didn't warn you."

Irritation was immediate and blanketed over her. Sam didn't know if it was his tone or the way he thought that he had a right to tell her what to do. She'd been living an entire life on her own terms. She wasn't about to have someone telling her what she could and could not do.

She stewed about it the entire day.
At four o'clock that afternoon, Sam went over to her mother's. She knew dinner wouldn't be ready yet, but she was looking forward to spending time with her.

Sam recalled what her mother said about being an agent. Mother had commented on more than one occasion about Sam or her agency not representing her. Sam certainly hadn't meant anything by it. In fact, she'd offered to refer her manuscripts to another agent house that represented the erotic romance genre, and Mother had acted insulted. Maybe she didn't understand that Sam couldn't represent her. Maybe she should talk to Mother about it. If they cleared the air, it might help with things between them. It couldn't hurt, could it?

Sam stepped onto the porch and heard the yelling before her hand touched the antique brass doorknob.

"Now, calm down" came Mother's voice. "Maybe it's not what you think."

A loud sob came from the kitchen. Sam hurried inside to see Theresa and Mother sitting at the kitchen island.

"Don't be so naïve!" Theresa pressed a tissue to her eyes. "It's exactly what I—" Theresa saw Sam and stopped mid-sentence. "What are you doing here?"

"I can't come over?"

"You could have knocked first." Theresa loudly blew her nose. Mascara ran a black river down each eye. No doubt one of the kids got a B in geometry or something.
Whatever this was, it didn't matter. Years of irritation boiled up in her. She was suddenly glad Theresa was crying, for whatever reason it was this time. She didn't care.

Helping herself to a glass in the cupboard, Sam opened the refrigerator and poured herself a glass of iced tea. Mother always had iced tea in a pitcher from as far back as she could remember, and during summer she always soaked in a leaf or two of the mint growing in her garden. It was no longer summer and today there was no mint. The tea was rather strong for her taste. Sam hadn't recalled it being disappointing.

"Last I knew," she said as she took a long drink of tea. "This was Mom's house. Not yours."

Theresa looked at her as if she was going to attack. Sam was instantly reminded of their teenage years and some of the fights becoming physical. Theresa had shoved Sam down the stairs in one of their matches. It was a wonder they were both living to tell about it.

But now they weren't teenagers, and they should be able to get along. Sam immediately regretted her mouth. It had been a long, difficult day, and her temper was short.

She sighed. "I'm sorry."

"Thank you, Sam." Mother added. "Theresa, your sister apologized."

"It's fine," Theresa mumbled.

"What's wrong?" Sam sat down beside her mother and across from Theresa.

"Shawn's leaving me."

"Oh, you don't know that!" Mother spoke up. "You haven't even talked to him yet." "She hasn't even talked to him." Mother looked at Sam.

"What happened?"

Mother shook her hand as if to brush the problem away. "Theresa and Shawn are having a marital…thing."

"A thing, Mom. A thing!" Theresa glared at their mother then turned to Sam and burst into tears. "Shawn cheated on me!"

Sam couldn't have been more shocked. This was the first bad thing that had ever happened to Theresa. Sam suddenly felt guilty for all the jealousy she'd felt over the years. Sam thought they'd been happy, would always be happy. That was just how Theresa's life seemed. On the outside.

Sam hugged her sister. Strangely, it was genuine, not the slightest bit awkward. "It will be okay. Maybe it was just a misunderstanding."

"I saw…things in our bedroom."

"Things?" Sam had never seen such a look of protection on her mother's face. "What things?"

"A condom." Theresa blew her nose. "We don't use them. I'm on the pill. And I wanted to have another kid!"

Theresa broke into a fit of sobs and hiccups. She mumbled something else in her tissue, but Sam couldn't make it out. "What sweetie?"

"I said she's still in school!"

"Ew…" Sam was mortified.

Mother echoed the sentiment. "I'll have him arrested!"

Theresa shook her head. "Not school as in pedophile. She's in college. She's twenty-one. Can you even believe it? Shawn's forty!"

"Oh." Sam felt a little better about the situation, such as it was. She recalled seeing Shawn talking to a group of women at Aunt Jean's funeral. She'd heard him ask a striking redhead if he could buy her a drink sometime. She didn't think anything of it at the time. Sure, it was a total pickup line, but Shawn had Theresa. Beautiful, smart, perfect. Could Shawn have been hitting on the redhead? No...maybe? Maybe this hadn't been his first affair. Just the first time he'd gotten caught. Sam didn't know how to help her sister. She could find Shawn and kick him in the balls, but that probably wouldn't solve anything.

It was a strange feeling wanting to help Theresa. It felt...kind of good. What family should be.

"What are you going to do?" Mother placed a hand over Theresa's.

Theresa sniffled. "I don't know."

"Don't go back there." Mother's voice was stern. "Bring the kids and stay here."

"No." Theresa squared her shoulders. "He's the one who's leaving. He cheated on me, and that's my house."

Sam had never seen her sister so determined. It suited her well.

CHAPTER NINE

Sam couldn't sleep that night. Lying in bed, thoughts of Theresa and what she could do to help plagued her. She looked at the digital clock on the nightstand. Midnight. Certainly too late to call anyone, even though it was likely Theresa was still up. Theresa had left Mother's determined to confront Shawn and put an end to her marriage. Shawn was the fault of everything, and she was equally dead set to take him to the cleaners.

Good for her.

Sam wondered if Ian would ever cheat on a woman. Before, when he'd been the kind of man who had stood her up so many years ago, maybe, but now, now she doubted it. Now she imagined he'd be the kind of man who would stay loyal to a woman despite any obstacle.

The thought surprised her. Certainly there was no future with Ian.

Ian was doing the best he could. He was a good person dealt a difficult hand. She had no right to judge him. Thoughts of Chet came to mind. She wondered why he came all the way here. He was an insurance agent and traveled often but would have no reason to come all the way out to Cold Springs. The last thing Sam had said to him was that they should go their separate ways because it was obvious the relationship wasn't going anywhere and Chet had agreed. But they'd remained in contact. Revealing nothing really, just a casual acquaintance, nothing more than two casual friends, if even that. Did he miss her?

Sam picked up her cell phone. This was a mistake. Sam would be making her mother very happy hooking up with Chet, but in her experience, pleasing Mother was never a good thing, and she was going against Ian. Sort of, and right now that seemed like a very good thing.
She picked up the receiver and dialed Chet's number.

~ * ~

Sam sat across the table listening to Chet go on about his work. He was stalling and she didn't understand why. It was one thing to be proud of one's job and all the accomplishments that went along with it, but Chet was overdoing it.

He wanted something.

Chet had called her back almost immediately after she'd left the message on his voicemail last night. Now, as she waited for the server to bring the check, she wondered about what she still had to do at the diner tonight. It was already past eight. She should get back and see about some of the accounting work waiting for her.

The waiter approached their table. "Would you like to see our dessert menu?"

"Sure."

"Just the check please." Sam cleared her throat.

"You can't go so soon." Chet's look was accusing. "We just got here."

"I really have a lot of work to do before tomorrow."

"Sam." Chet took her hand, holding it a little too forcibly for comfort. "We need to talk."

"Isn't that what you've been doing?" She couldn't hide her irritation. "Why did you come all the way out here? I know it's not to talk about your work."

"I made a mistake. I miss you, Sam."

He surprised her. She hadn't expected this. In all their texts and e-mails he'd never once even hinted at missing her. Why now?

"You can't be happy here. Look at this town. There's nothing here to offer you."

"My family's here."

"Your family's always been here. We can come here and visit just like you've always done." He ran a hand through his hair then smiled.
We?
Chet had never addressed the two of them with the term we before. A month ago, Sam would have thought it was a promise of something wonderful yet to come. Now she found it annoying and somewhat controlling, and it took her completely off guard. "I'm happy right here, Chet."

The waiter brought the check. They both reached for it at once. Chet's fingers brushed hers and she pulled back. She recalled walks in Central Park with him, where they'd spent time hand in hand. Not many walks but there had been a couple. Sam didn't want him touching her now.

"I can get half," Sam spoke up. She suddenly didn't want to owe him, not even for something as insignificant as dinner.

Chet pulled out his credit card. "No, I insist."

It bothered her that he was paying for her meal. She didn't exactly know why. Maybe because she was so used to picking up the tab when she used to take authors out for business lunches. Maybe because it had been so long since she'd been on a real date.

Real date? She thought of Ian and the barbeque they'd had at his apartment. That hadn't felt like a date. Instead it had felt like two friends enjoying the day together. There had been no awkwardness, no feelings of insecurity that came with being with someone you didn't know very well. She had just…enjoyed herself and enjoyed Ian's company.

She wondered what Ian was doing right now.

The waiter ran Chet's card through and brought it back for his signature. Sam stood and headed toward the door. Chet trailed behind her.

In the parking lot, she headed toward Chet's rental car, a dark gray Lincoln with black leather interior. Only the best for Chet. Most everyone in Cold Springs drove a pickup truck. The car stuck out like a sore thumb.

"Thank you for dinner." She hurriedly got in after he beeped the alarm and fastened her seatbelt. She was in a hurry to get away and had the most incredible urge to just walk home. Chet got in but made no move to start the engine. "Sam—"

"No." She didn't want to hear what he had to say. Before coming to Cold Springs, it would have meant everything, but now so much had changed. Chet, New York, it all seemed so small and unimportant now. She didn't have the same needs anymore. "I really have to get back home. Maybe some other time."

"Some other time?" He gave a small, annoyed laugh. "Sam, I came all this way for you. I want you to come back. I'm ready to settle down. I'm ready to take the next step with you."

He took her hand. Sam stared down at his fingers intertwined with hers. His hands were soft, his nails manicured. Ian's were calloused from hard labor, his nails bitten or torn off from worry that came from not knowing where he would get his next month's money or his next meal for that matter.

Sam pulled her hand away. "Chet, I appreciate you. You've always been a friend to me, but—"

"But?" He sighed. "There's someone else."

"I have a place here."

"This stupid diner?"

"It's not stupid." She immediately felt the need to defend herself, her aunt, and everything the diner represented.

"It is, Sam. You have a life in New York. We have a life."

"We were acquaintances, Chet. We dated. It was good while it lasted, but like you said, you didn't see it going any further."

Chet was silent for a moment, and Sam wondered if he was letting his own words she'd used against him sink in. Finally, he said, "Well, I was wrong."

"Hey," she rested her hand over his, "it's okay."

"It's someone else, isn't it?"

Sam thought of Ian. It was and so much more. Ian was everything to what Cold Springs meant. He was everything.

Chet pulled his hand away. "That's just great. You know, I thought we had something. I thought we meant something."

"We did. I mean we do. We will always be friends."

"Friends." He laughed bitterly. "It's all cut and dry for you, isn't it?"

Sam didn't know what to say. She didn't want to hurt him, but clearly she had changed. They had both changed, and there was nothing more to say. "Can you take me home, please?"

Chet pushed the automatic door lock. Sam tried the door anyway, but it wouldn't budge. Her heart rate tripped beats. She remembered the years in the city and the safety precautions she always took. She hadn't taken any here because it was Cold Springs and he was familiar, safe.

"Let me out."

Chet leaned forward as if he was going to kiss her. "Chet, stop!"

Make a scene.

Before she could think, Sam let out a bloodcurdling scream. Chet jumped. He unlocked the doors, and she bolted. He called after her, but thankfully didn't seem to be following.

Sam sprinted up the sidewalk, past her mother's house, and didn't stop until she was on Main Street. Jean's Diner came into view. Sam had left the outside light on, and it was like a beacon of safety.

Aunt Jean was always like that. Like coming home.

She hurried to the door. Her hands shook so badly she could barely slip her key in the lock. She let herself in, locking it behind her and flipped on every light in the place.
She sank to the floor, shaking uncontrollably. A rap on the door nearly sent her into orbit. If Chet followed her, she'd call his—

Ian.

She hurriedly unlocked and opened the door.

"I drove by and saw all the lights on. I thought something was— what's wrong?"

Sam threw herself into his arms. Tears came fast and hard. Chet hadn't done anything, she really didn't know if he would have—would he have?—but it didn't matter. He'd scared her. She was so stupid to trust, to think nothing would happen in such a small town. To trust someone just because he was familiar.

Sam told Ian every detail of her night. All the stress and the fear of the past few weeks came rushing forth like a tidal wave. Ian was warmth and comfort, and she felt safe with him.

"If he hurt you—"

"No," Sam interrupted, both shocked and flattered by his sudden protectiveness. "Let it go. It's not worth getting yourself in trouble over."

"I'm spending the night here with you in case he comes here."

Sam nodded. Not that she thought Chet would dare after that banshee scream she let out near his eardrum. No matter, Sam was okay with Ian never leaving.

Where had that thought come from? And furthermore, what could she hope to do with it? There was no future to be had with Ian. She would never have the white picket fence and large successful family like—

Like Theresa? Who was crying her eyes out because Shawn had cheated on her?

Sam couldn't picture Ian ever cheating on her, simply because he'd been through hell and back and most likely couldn't imagine doing the same to someone else.

Ian tugged off his sweatshirt, the white tee he wore beneath riding up with it to reveal the nastiest looking scar Sam had ever seen. Over a foot long of twisted, puckered flesh trailed from the right side of his back, curving toward his stomach. Too crooked to be from a surgical procedure. An accident?
Sam looked up to see him watching her, his expression unreadable. No accident.
Images of prison riots formed in her mind. She pictured Ian being attacked with some sort of homemade weapon, something so primitive and wicked that it tore open such a gash in his side.

Ian ran a hand through his hair. Sam had the urge to do the same to it.

Her entire life she'd never been one to act upon urges, but she needed to touch him. Needed to comfort him, do something in recognition, in mourning for the years wasted, for the violence he'd endured behind bars. She reached up, barely caressing the spot where his hairline was beginning to recede slightly. A few fine hairs were starting to gray. Ian would be a man to age gracefully, she could tell.

Ian closed his eyes, leaned into her touch. He gave a slow intake of breath and the urge to kiss him was suddenly too much. Standing on her tiptoes, she rested her hands on his shoulders and lightly touched his lips with her own. His kiss was gentle, reserved, restrained out of respect for her.

Ian rested his forehead against hers. "If he ever touches you like that again, I'll kill him."
Chet. Right. She'd forgotten.
"Let it go, please. It's not worth getting yourself into trouble over."

"I'm spending the night here with you," he said again, as if he expected her to give him a fight, but she was okay with that.

"Promise me you won't go near him." Sam pulled his face to look at her. The situation reminded her of his fight with his sister's boyfriend and how he'd ended up in jail in the first place. Protecting someone.

"I won't touch him."

"I mean it." She swallowed. "I need you here."

"I'm sure you could find another cook."

"I'm not talking about a cook." Sam had never told a man how she felt. Maybe because she'd never had much opportunity. She'd never met one that made her feel much of anything, and she'd always been too busy working to find one. Now she was still working and she'd found one. She couldn't imagine wanting to find anyone else.

When had it happened? She couldn't recall an exact moment. Little things. The way she could depend on him. How he was protective of her. How she could talk to him. The things Burt said about him. It all added up to one very big thing.

She loved him.

Pulling his face to hers, she kissed him full and squarely the way he deserved to be kissed. No reserve, holding nothing back. When they both came up for air, they were breathing heavy.

He grinned. "What was that for?"

"I'm glad you're here."

"I should come over more often."

"You should." She took his hand and led him toward the stairwell that led to the upstairs apartment.

"Wait." He stopped. "Are you sure about this?"

Sam gave him her most seductive kiss yet. "This is the surest I've felt since moving to Cold Springs."

~ * ~

Ian couldn't work at the diner the next day. He had to give Jake Sanderson an estimate for repairing his barn roof then finish up a siding job outside of town. He couldn't keep his thoughts off Sam. He loved her, probably had always loved her.

Feelings of protection welled up inside him. In an unexpected way it felt as if something bad was about to happened because he felt this happy. His whole life, every time things were going right, the other shoe fell. Right before he went to the pen he'd had a full football scholarship and had lost it. Now he had Sam back. He'd first lost her from his own stupidity, and he wasn't about to do it again.

Driving through Pulaski, he purchased supplies at the local hardware, passed by Townsend's Secondhand Shop and stopped. Displayed in the front window was a woman's wedding set. The wedding ring was a plain gold ring, but the engagement ring was a diamond. He knew that because it resembled one like his mother wore. She'd never removed hers even after his dad died. Mom had called it a princess cut. This ring wasn't very big. Ian had no idea how many carets it was, but it was pretty. Small and pretty. Just like Sam.

It was probably the second most impulsive thing he'd ever done — the first being murder — but he went in and paid the owner two hundred fifty dollars cash and came out the owner of a secondhand wedding set.

His heart pounded in his chest. He didn't even know Sam's finger size, didn't even know if she wanted to get married, let alone to him, didn't even know — wasn't it bad luck to buy a used wedding ring?

He jumped in his truck, stuffed the box in the glove compartment and got the hell out of there before someone from Cold Springs saw what he'd just done.

~ * ~

The diner was packed. Chrissy had called in sick, but reluctantly came in when Martha left on her break and literally went to Chrissy's apartment and brought her in. Chrissy was nearly in tears.

"She just barged into my apartment." Chrissy wrapped the strings of her apron twice around her lithe waist and tied it on the side. "She's so rude. Ben was really mad. It was so embarrassing."
"Ben?" Sam was pouring coffee as fast as people drank. She started another pot.
"Yeah. Ben Towles. I've been seeing him. He's thirty. I know he's older, but he's really cute." She giggled, flashing Sam large, wide-set doe eyes. "Okay, I know I wasn't really sick. I'm sorry."

Sam wiped down the counter as Chrissy walked away to wait tables. She nearly bumped into Martha who was pouring Burt's coffee as two older men greeted him and took the last empty seats at the counter.

Burt turned their way. "Have a seat, Fred, Bill. Coffee's on the house today."

"You can't do that." Martha stopped in her tracks. She set the coffee pot on the counter, slapped two palms down and glared at Burt like a sumo wrestler ready to take action. "You have no right giving out free anything. Coffee's normal price, gentlemen. Same as always."

Burt looked undefeated. "Seems like Fred and Bill come here every morning, they should get something on the house."

"They get fine food at a reasonable price. That's their something."

"And when Chrissy's here they get good service."

Martha narrowed her eyes. "Sam, we have a problem."

"It's too busy to be worrying about this right now," Sam called over her shoulder as she sped past with an armload of breakfasts.

Martha slammed her fist on the counter. "That's it. It's him or me. I'm not putting up with this — or her," she pointed toward Chrissy, "anymore!"

Sam came back toward the counter after she passed out the meals. "Martha, don't do this."

"This is unacceptable working practice. You got a waitress who cares more about snagging her next bed partner than she does working, customers who think they can get everything for free, and—"

"I'm sorry, but I'm not throwing customers out."

"Then I'll leave."

"Martha," Sam called.

"Good riddance," Burt said. Fred and Bill grinned from ear to ear.

Sam slammed the pot down. "Then you can serve coffee." She threw an apron at Burt. She went after Martha, catching her right before she stormed to her car. "Martha, please. Don't do this. I know things are less than ideal, but give it some time. I'm new at this. Give me a break. Please. I'll make it better. I don't know how yet, but give me some time. I promise I'll do right by you."

Martha turned to face her. Years of experience glared at her, and Sam felt like a sudden failure. "Besides, if you go, who will Burt have to fight with?"

A hint of a smirk lightened Martha's face. "I had a fight with my husband this morning. It was over the kitchen light over the sink. He promises to fix things and they never get done. I remind him and I'm the constant nag."

"I'm sorry."

"I'm not." Martha slid her car keys back in her pocket. "But I won't leave you. Let's go."

Relief washed over Sam and she followed Martha back to the diner. "Thank you."

When they got inside, Burt was making rounds with the coffeepot, proudly wearing the apron that Sam had thrown at him. He carried a fistful of dollar bills and Mrs. Mills, Cold Springs's postmaster general, slapped him on the rear as he passed her table. "Sexiest waiter I've ever seen." She whistled, sending the table of old hens cackling at an ear splitting level.

Martha and Sam went after the tables, waiting on customers left and right. Panic gradually left Sam as she got into the fast-paced groove. She'd just started to think everything was going to be all right, when Chet Tyler walked through the door.

"Hi, Sam. Can we talk?"

"I'm too busy, Chet." She started pouring coffee. "If you're here for breakfast, have a seat, and Chrissy will be happy to serve you. Otherwise, we have nothing to say to one another."

"C'mon, Sam. Don't be like that."

Chet reached out and grabbed Sam's arm, the same arm Sam held the coffeepot with. Instinctively, Sam jerked back, spilling half the pot of hot coffee all over Mr. and Mrs. Newlander, Mother's next door neighbors.

"Oh my God!" Sam didn't have time to react. Misses Newlander screamed, as scalding coffee slopped on her arms and shoulders.

Sam set the pot on the nearest table, launched herself into the kitchen to grab ice and towels as a cold compress. She quickly gave them to the Newlanders. "I'm so sorry."

"Someone call 911!" Chet just stood there staring.

"This is all your fault!" someone told him.

"Yeah," Burt agreed. "I saw the whole thing."

"She never would have dumped it if he hadn't grabbed her arm," Steve Sanders added. He was sitting at the counter next to Burt.

Chet shrugged. "I didn't do it on purpose."

"You could still call for help!" Burt shouted.

It didn't matter because Martha was already talking to the 911 dispatcher.
"Yes. We have applied ice. Yes. Jean's Diner. On Main. Yes. Thank you." She hung up the phone. "The EMT is on the way."

Sam knelt beside the couple. She couldn't imagine the pain she'd caused the both of them. They were each in their eighties, and she'd known them since she was little. Mr. Newlander had a bad hip and required the aid of a cane to walk. He claimed he was uninjured, but the skin on his hand was bright red, and Sam pleaded with him to keep the ice applied to the burn. Mrs. Newlander had received the worst of the injuries. Her arm was red and angry blisters were already beginning to form. "I'm so sorry, Mrs. Newlander."

"It was an accident, dear."

"No, I should have been more careful."

"The EMT will be here soon," Martha said.

"I don't need it," Mrs. Newlander assured. "A little ice and it will be fine."

"I'd feel better if you got checked out."

"They're here," someone shouted. "Clear the way!"

Sam stepped aside as the EMTs came through. They checked the Newlanders' vitals, asked them questions. Each insisted they were fine, but Sam finally convinced Mr. Newlander to call their daughter to come take him to the hospital where they were taking his wife.

Sam watched them leave, heard others discussing amongst themselves the possibility of the Newlanders suing her, of bringing a case against the diner. Sam didn't care. She would pay the bill. She just wanted them to be all right. Nothing else mattered.

Chet came up behind her. "We need to talk, Sam."

"Chet, just get out."

CHAPTER TEN

The diner was slow the next morning. Sam hadn't slept from worrying about the Newlanders. Mrs. Newlander had called her when she got home, saying her injuries were mild and she was given an antibiotic, bandaged, and had to make an appointment with her general practitioner in a few days to check for infection. Sam was thankful and as soon as they were open had called the florist to have a get-well bouquet sent over to her.

Her mother came in early. "Hi, Mom."
Sam poured her a cup of coffee, pushed the box of fresh doughnuts her way. Mother took a frosted jelly pastry.
"How did the date with Chet go?" Mother whispered over the counter loud enough for customers on either side of her to hear.

"I don't want to talk about it."

"That well?"

Two women and a boy about ten years old came in. Sam grabbed three menus and headed to the table they went to. "Good morning. Coffee?"

"Yes, please." They both chimed.

"What can I get you?" Sam directed her attention to the boy. His eyes were bright with dark features, and he seemed bored by the whole scene.

"Soda," he muttered.

"He'll have milk," the younger woman, Sam assumed his mother, corrected.

"White?"

"Please."

Sam took another glance at the woman. She looked vaguely familiar, but Sam couldn't place her. She was bringing them their drinks when it dawned on her. Ian's sister, Roxanne, and his mother. The boy must be Teddy, who hadn't even been born when Ian had been incarcerated.

"Roxanne Woods." Sam set down beverages. "Do you remember me? Samantha Stone. We went to the same high school. I was in the same graduating class with your brother, Ian…actually."

They all looked at her as if she'd said something incredibly rude. It was as if they were expecting some sort of shoe to drop with the mention of Ian's name. Sam recalled what Ian had said about how strained his relationship was with them.

"You probably don't remember me." Sam cleared her throat. "That's okay. It was a long time ago. Ian and I used to be friends — are still friends, so I just thought you'd remember me."

Sam felt heat rise to her cheeks. Pure word vomit was pouring out of her mouth, and she couldn't stop it. She wanted to defend Ian to these people, his family, who were supposed to be in his corner, were supposed to love him unconditionally no matter what he did.

"I remember you." Roxanne's tone was curt.

Ian's mother smiled. "You've done a nice job with the diner."

"Thank you." Sam smiled, feeling slightly relieved. Ian's mother appeared uncomfortable. Sam wondered if she should apologize or keep her mouth shut. "Well, thank you for coming in. What can I get you?"
They ordered breakfast, and Sam headed to the kitchen.

"Did you hear her?" Roxanne whispered when Sam's back was turned. "She's still friends with him."

Moments later, Sam delivered food to a table, wondering if she should say something to Ian about his family being here. Did they know he worked here? Somehow Sam doubted it. She wanted to do something to get them talking again. It was none of her business, but it wasn't right. Families needed one another.

She went to Ian, who was busy flipping a pile of home fries. He smiled and stole a kiss. "You smell nice."

"I smell like diner food."

His smile was infectious. "I like diner food."

"Your mom and sister are here."

All lightheartedness left his face. "What do they want?"

"Breakfast." She handed him their order slip.

Without a word, Ian pinned it up overhead and started the order.

"Are you going to speak to them?"

"No."

"Why not?"

"Let it go, Sam."

"Why not just try? Maybe—"

"I said no."

His tone stung as if he'd slapped her. Tears welled and she hated herself for being so sensitive. She should have just minded her own business.

She wondered what it would take to knock down the walls he had built around his heart but doubted if she could, if anyone could. And right now she was tired of trying.
Without a word, she went back to working. The diner was getting full when she noticed Ian taking his family's breakfast out to them. Sam was waiting on the table next to them when she heard him whisper. "Hi, Mom. Roxanne. Hi, Ted."

His mother's expression was total shock. "Ian." Pushing her chair out, she stood, cautiously hugged him. It was almost as if asking permission. Ian melted into her embrace. There was no hate. Just regret and worry, and something far more. Love.

Roxanne, on the other hand, made no move toward her brother. She looked down at her place, refusing to acknowledge him. His mother sat back down, pulled out the chair beside her. "Sit."

"I can't. I'm working."

"You work here?"

Ian nodded. "I do this, and I started my own construction business."

Ian touched Teddy's arm. "Hey, buddy."

"Don't touch him."

"Roxanne." Ian's mother kept her voice low.

"What, Mom?" Roxanne pushed her plate away. "You're just going to sit there and pretend like nothing happened?"

"Something happened, Roxy." Ian kept his voice even.

Everyone was starting at them now. Ian seemed to realize it too, at the same time he glanced up and saw Sam watching him. Correction: Sticking her nose in his business again.

Sam quickly made herself scarce. All the while she felt Ian's glare boring into her back.

~ * ~

Ian was the last person Sam expected to see at her door that night. Ian didn't knock. Just let himself in with the key Sam had given him, which he'd been reluctant to take, but Sam had insisted to prove her trust in him. He stood in the middle of her tiny living room like a giant. He didn't say anything. He didn't have to. Sam stood, and Ian opened his arms.

There was no need for words. She knew he hadn't meant to be harsh. He had been scared but he had faced his fears anyway. Closing her eyes against his chest, she sighed as he gently stroked her hair.

"I'm sorry."

"I know."

"You were just trying to help." He kissed the top of her head.

"It's okay."

"No." He sighed. "It's not. Every time you try to help me, I push it away. Every single time."

Sam stepped back and stared at him. His expression was determined. "Well, maybe recognizing it is the first step to changing it."

He smiled, relief immediate in his expression. "Maybe."

He pulled her close and kissed her. "I'm going to change. I promise."

"Well, don't change too much." She pressed herself against him, feeling his arousal against her. "I kind of like some parts of you as they are."

~ * ~

At six o'clock the following evening, Ian stood on his mother's doorstep, his heart hammering in his chest. It wasn't supposed to be like this. He wasn't supposed to feel like a stranger near his family. It wasn't the same here. He hadn't grown up in this home. That had ended in the divorce. Marriages had a way of ending after a son went to jail.

He cautiously rapped in the door.

After a few moments, his mother opened the door. Her hair was styled in a modern blunt cut. It had grayed considerably since he'd gone to jail. He'd noticed it immediately when seeing her at the diner.

Her face was a mask of surprise and something else. Shock? Sadness? "Ian."

"Hi, Mom."

"You came."

Had she thought he would stand her up? He had called yesterday and she had invited him to dinner after all. "Of course, I came. Can I come in?"

"Yes." She stepped aside and motioned for him to come in as if at a loss for words. "You thought I wouldn't come?"

"I wasn't sure. I mean, I don't know how busy you are nowadays." She smiled then turned serious. "I don't know you anymore. I want to know you."

Something broke in him just then. He was surprised, stunned, shocked. She still wondered about him, perhaps still cared. Maybe, just maybe, he could have some assemblage of family back. "I want to know you, too."

With that, Ian reached forward and hugged her. She had lost considerable weight since he'd last remembered. She was never overweight, but now she seemed too thin.

The hug was warm and strong, and his mother held him back with a fierceness that promised a lifetime of forgiveness. Her shoulders sagged and shuddered.

"It's all right, Mom. I'm sorry. I'm sorry for everything. I'm so sorry."

"I should have been there for you." She sobbed. "I went to see you, but they said you didn't want to see me."

"I didn't want you in that place." He squeezed her tightly, her sobs ripping his heart out. Regret tore at him. He'd thought he was doing the right thing at the time. He'd never wanted her in that place. She was too good. No mother should have to see her son in jail. He should have granted her the visits. He had no right denying her.

"What kind of mother doesn't visit her son?"

"What kind of son goes to jail for manslaughter?" he was quick to answer. He held her tightly. "I wouldn't have wanted you in that place. It was my fault. Everything was my fault."

She pulled back, and wiped her eyes with the back of her hand. "I made tuna noodle casserole. That used to be your favorite."

"It's still my favorite."

She started crying again. Ian put an arm around her. "Don't cry, Mom. It's okay."

"I'll try." She smiled and gave a nervous laugh, and the tears started again. "It's just that it's been so long."

"Ten years."

"Ten years," she repeated as if confirming it to himself.

"Here," Ian took the casserole and proceeded to help her set the table. "I don't know where you keep things, but I want to help you out."

She was frail, too thin. She wasn't like he remembered. No one and nothing was.

He'd ended up telling her everything from his trial to the endless days in prison to what parole was like to how he'd gotten reacquainted with Sam when his mother had asked how he'd felt about Sam.

Ian had spilled out everything as if he'd been sharing details with his mother for years when in fact this was the only close conversation they'd ever had in his life. It felt good. Beyond good. He had family. He no longer felt like an outcast. He had a sense of belonging, purpose. Even his parole officer, whom he'd had a meeting with this morning, had noticed, had said speaking to his family — even though his sister was less than receptive to him — had been a progressive move forward. Family support was one of the most important tools to staying clean on the outside, he'd said. And that felt good. Damn good.

And it was all because of Sam.

~ * ~

Ian arrived at the diner a little before 9 a.m., just after his parole meeting. Parking his truck in the back alley, he entered the diner through the storage room. He heard the shouting all the way from outside. Ian hurried to the dining room where Chrissy and Martha stood in the middle of the room. The place was packed, and they were ringside and Sam was the referee.

"I can't believe you're not going to fire her!"

"Martha, please stop." Sam was pouring coffee and trying to calm Martha at the same time. "She didn't mean to mess up the orders. We're all busy and overworked. Mistakes happen."

"And they keep happening! She doesn't learn. She's too busy talking about her boyfriend and doesn't listen to what the customers are ordering."

"And how is that different from you telling us about your argument with Bill this morning?" Burt didn't look up for his breakfast. "It's not Chrissy's fault that your husband's an asshole."

Customers stared, wide-eyed and shocked.

Chrissy burst into tears and ran into the kitchen.

"Chrissy!" Burt called. "Chrissy, don't be upset. Poor little girl. I don't know if I should go after her or just let her calm down."
"So Chrissy's taken now." Fred sat at the counter drinking his coffee thoughtfully. He shook his head.
"Yep." Tom forked a huge pile of home fries and stuck them in his mouth. "Here I thought she liked me the whole time."

Ian caught Sam and quickly gave her a peck on the cheek. "Mornin'."

"Hi." She smiled.
Her smile always made his heart skip a beat. "I talked to Mom."

"Yeah?" She smiled as she went down the line pouring coffee. "How'd it go?"

Ian made more coffee. "Good. Really well, actually."

"That's great. We'll talk more tonight, okay?"

"Okay." Ian brushed a lock of Sam's hair back over her ear. Sam had enough on her plate with running the diner. She didn't need this mess with Martha and Chrissy. He wished he could do something for her to smooth her life out.
"Hi, Ian."
Ian turned to see his sister, Roxy and her son, Teddy, standing by the front door.
"Hi, Roxy." He approached them. He knelt and smiled at Teddy. "Hi, Ted."
"Hi."
"What are you doing here?" He stood eye level with his sister.
"We came for breakfast." Roxy's smile was tentative, cautious.

"Well, c'mon." Ian grabbed two menus and motioned her to follow. "There's a table back here. Can I get you some coffee?"

"Sure, but can you sit with us?" She removed Teddy's jacket and sat.

Sam was watching him as she waited tables. He saw Roxy's wide-eyed look of encouragement and reluctantly sat across from her. Nerves tightened. Last time he'd seen his sister, she had nothing but scorn for him. Now…why the change?

"Mom said you came over the other day."

And there it was. "I did," he answered.

"She never gave up on you." Tears welled in her eyes, and she frantically brushed them away. "Not like I did."

Ian couldn't resist the urge to grab her hand. He squeezed her fingers with his, and to his surprise, she caught him in an embrace. "I'm sorry for everything."

"I'm sorry too. I've wanted to make peace with you for a while. I was so messed up and confused about everything. Then I was too ashamed to talk to you." The diner was packed, but Ian didn't care. He hugged his sister tightly, feeling the weight immediate lift from him. For the first time in so many years, he wondered if everything would be okay. Maybe…just maybe.

"Teddy, this is your Uncle Ian I told you about." Teddy smiled. At him. "You own this place?"

"No, bud. I work here. You get anything you want for breakfast. It's on me."

"Maybe you two can go to the zoo or something sometime together," Roxy offered.

"You mean it?"

"Today?"

Ian and Teddy spoke at once, and Roxy laughed.

"Yes, I mean it, but not today, Ted. Uncle Ian has to work."

"Awww!"

"How about this Sunday?" Ian ruffled Teddy's hair. "I'm free then."

"Okay."

He turned to Roxy, gave her a quick hug.

"Thank you. You don't know what this means to me."

"Maybe I do."

Ian was about to go back to the kitchen when Pete Maitland's voice boomed above every other conversation. "Mom? Mom!"

Sam's mother, who had been sitting at the counter, was now slumped, about ready to fall off her stool. Sam held her as she melted to the floor.

Time stopped as Ian leapt over the counter and caught Madelaine's head and cradled it to prevent her from slamming her skull on the hard tile. "Call 911! Madelaine? Madelaine!"

Madelaine was clutched her chest. "Hurts."

"Don't speak. It'll be okay. We're gonna get you help. Just hang in there." Customers had gathered around him like gawkers at a sideshow. "Get back. Give her space!"

Sam pushed them aside. "Step back. Please."

Chrissy pushed through the crowd. "Oh my God! That's Sam's mom. What happened?"

"Don't make her talk."

"Get him away from her," Ian heard someone shout, "before he kills again."

Ian tried not to panic. He tried not to imagine how scared Sam must be. Just exactly how old was she? Sixty? Why wasn't help coming faster?

He felt her neck for a pulse, but his hands were shaking too badly to register one. In prison he had taken a CPR class. At the time he'd just took it for something to do, but now. How many presses on the chest was it again?

"Somebody stop him!"

He tilted Madelaine's head and lifted her chin. Pressing two fingers in her mouth, he felt for an obstruction but found nothing.

Thirty. Start with thirty chest compressions.

"Didn't anyone call 911?"

"They're on their way," Tom Benson answered.

"What the hell's taking them so long?"

Ian felt Sam's hand on his shoulder. "Save her, Ian. Please."

~ * ~

"I'm sorry. Due to HIPAA laws, I can't tell you about her condition. You'll have to wait for her family or she will have to consent herself."

Sam came around the corner to meet Ian. He'd phoned her that he was coming to the hospital. She found him leaning against the counter of the reception desk, getting nowhere with the woman running the switchboard.

The receptionist's look was apologetic. "I'm sorry."

"It's okay. He's with me."

Ian rushed her, grabbing her hand and squeezing so hard, it hurt. "How is she?"

"She hasn't woken up yet. They have her hooked up to so many tubes." Sam fought the urge to cry. She didn't know what to think about anything, except that she was exhausted. It had been a terrible day, and the only thing Sam wanted was to turn back the clock.

Chrissy had volunteered to keep the diner open, said it would keep her mind off things. Chrissy wasn't good with money so Sam had called Martha in just in case. Hopefully they weren't fighting.

She wondered what Aunt Jean would think of all this. Most likely, she would laugh off the little things, claiming they were all little things. Aunt Jean would be worried sick about Mother. As it were, Mother was all alone, and if anything happened to her…

They walked down the long, cold hall to the room where Mother lay hooked up to all sorts of tubes and wires. The nurses had warned Sam of the shock she would feel upon seeing her like that for the first time. It hadn't gotten any easier throughout the afternoon.

Except Mother's eyes were now open.

Sam rushed to her side. Theresa was there and sat on one side of the bed. "She just woke up."

A hot tear welled and flowed down Sam's cheek. She smiled, took her hand that didn't have an IV inserted in it. "How are you feeling?"

"I'm alive."

Ian stood over the bed. Mother stared at him, her eyes wide and questioning. "Y-you saved my life."

"You scared the hell out of me."

"I scared the hell out of me, too." Mother raised her voice. "All these damn doctors want to do is stick me full of needles and give me a bunch of pills."

"They said it wasn't a heart attack. Angina." Theresa's expression was thoughtful, as if she wanted to ease her worry.

"That's wonderful…that it wasn't an actual heart attack." Sam breathed a sigh of relief. It suddenly dawned on her just how poorly Mother took care of herself. She ate muffins or bagels with real cream cheese, not the fat free kind, nearly every morning. She was partially to blame for killing her. She was always pushing the fresh made doughnuts her way when she came in for coffee. "Not yet anyway. Which means a change in diet for you. It's turkey bacon and egg whites from now on. No more sweets."

"I'd rather die."

"You will if you keep on your diet." She was determined not to let her die. Maybe she could get her started on some sort of exercise program. Walking every morning or something.

"Glad you came back." She mumbled something else Sam couldn't understand. Her words were slurred, barely audible. She reached her hand out and Sam took it. Her grip was weak. Mother soon drifted off to sleep.

Sam kissed her forehead. "I'll come see you tomorrow, Mom."

Theresa stood. Mascara smeared down her face. She was just as exhausted as Sam. She took both of Ian's hands. "Thank you, Ian. You saved her life. I don't know what would have happened had you not done what you did."

"She would have been okay."

"No." Theresa shook her head. "She would have died, and you saved her."

Theresa fiercely hugged Ian, then as if remembering who he was, she pulled away. "Thank you for coming."

"Glad to help," Ian softly answered.

Sam hugged her sister goodbye. "I'll see you tomorrow."
"Thank you. I'll call you."
"Okay."

Ian waved as he placed a hand on the small of Sam's back to lead her out of the room. When they were far enough away, Sam gripped Ian's bicep. "Did you hear what Mom said? She said she was glad I came back to Cold Springs."

"So am I."

"She really said it. Maybe it was the drugs, but—"

"It wasn't the drugs. I think Theresa's glad you're back too. She needs you. They both need you. Now more than ever."

"More than ever," Sam repeated. She ran her hand down Ian's arm and intertwined her fingers with his. Everything would be different now. Perhaps she and Theresa would finally be close, like normal siblings. It wouldn't happen overnight, but now it seemed like there was a chance. And it felt good.

They reached Ian's truck, and Sam got in the driver's side and slid across the seat. Weeks of stress suddenly built up all at once. The constant work and worry about the bottom line, the problems with Mother and Theresa. Just when she thought she and Theresa were finally developing some sort of relationship, the rug had been pulled out from under them. And now Mother's health…lying there alone and connected to all those tubes. The same thing could happen to her, and Sam's family would never know how much she loved and appreciated them. Sam didn't want to lose them. Not when there was so much at stake. Life was short and precious.

She wasn't going to let that slip away.

Ian hopped in behind the wheel. "Hey, it'll be all right. Your mom's going to pull through."

"Tell me about your family," she demanded. She suddenly wanted to hear him talking about them, something she had never heard from him before.

"I already did."
"No, you told me about your sister and the bad things that happened. You never told me anything good. Tell me something good."

He was quiet for a long while. "My grandmother was always happy. I spent a lot of summers at her place upstate. She had a canoe. Us kids would use it and go all over the back streams with it. It was real tippy. We fished and caught snakes and frogs. I never forgot those summers."

Sam pictured Ian as a carefree child playing in the muddy waters and let the thought settle on her like a warm blanket. She laid her head on Ian's shoulder.

She must have drifted off to sleep or a deep, relaxed consciousness, but she drifted to thoughts of Ian, where they'd been and how far they'd come. Cold Springs had never held any expectations for love in Sam's world, but what she had with Ian, whatever it was that they shared in these few short weeks…love? Could you actually come to love someone so quickly?

Sam didn't want Ian to see her crying over this, over loneliness. Such a silly emotion. One in which she never gave a second thought before she came back to Cold Springs. She'd always been too busy, not that she wasn't busy now. This was difficult here in Cold Springs. She didn't want to be alone. She didn't want to look back on her life and have nothing but regret. Ian held her and she leaned into his embrace. He was rock solid and warm, his closeness promising that everything would be all right.

She reached for her purse for a tissue but remembered she'd left it at the diner in her rush to the hospital. Everything but tissues billowed out of his cup holders. She opened the glove compartment. A small black box popped out and fell onto the floor, hitting her big toe.

~ * ~

Ian had no idea what was going through Sam's mind as she bent to pick up the ring box. He shouldn't have left it there. He shouldn't have bought the ring period.

Suddenly the regret didn't matter anymore. It no longer mattered that this wasn't the right time or the right place. When would the timing or place ever be perfect? Life wasn't perfect.

Life was precious, and if you didn't grab hold of what you wanted, it would pass you by. He wanted Sam. In his life. Always.

He took the box from her and opened it. Sam's expression was questioning, confused. No doubt she didn't expect this. She would say it was too soon, that their relationship had been rushed. That they hadn't taken enough time and that it would never work. Too many expectations, too little stability. "Sam."

"Yes."

She made a statement, not a question. "Yes?"

Sam nodded. "Yes."

Ian laughed. "I haven't asked you yet."

"I don't care." Sam leaned into his arms.

"I love you." His voice broke. He kissed her neck, her ears, her eyes. "I've always loved you. Even when I was too stupid to realize it."

"Me too." Sam kissed him back. "And we were both too stupid to realize it."

EPILOGUE

Three months later

"You may kiss the bride."

Cheers bellowed out. Sam squeezed her eyes
shut as a hail of coffee beans pelted her and Ian.
Ian caught her in another embrace as they
laughed.
The diner was full of everyone they loved as
horns from cars drove by honking from the
marriage announcement Burt had hung over the
front door.

Sam and Ian were married in the center of Jean's
Diner. Much to Mother's and Theresa's
abhorrence that she didn't get married at
someplace fancy and expensive. Sam and Ian,
and of course Burt with all his friends thought it
was perfect. Mother made a full recovery — and
was miserable on a diet of turkey bacon and
fruits and veggies. Burt was the best man.
Theresa was the maid of honor, and Chrissy and
Martha were her bridesmaids.

Sam and Theresa had a long road to recovering
their relationship, and Theresa's divorce was still
pending based upon the multitude of material
possessions she and Shawn were contesting.

Mother gave her a long hug. She pressed her cheek against hers. "I think you're making a horrible mistake, but I hope I'm wrong." She stepped back, gave Ian a forced smile. "For your sake, I hope I'm very wrong."

Ian hugged her. "I promise to take excellent care of your daughter, Mom."

"Mrs. Stone."

"Mother!" Sam scolded.

"All right, how about Madelaine?" She glanced at Sam. "Oh, for heaven's sakes, Sam. I'm trying!"

"Thank you, Mom." Sam hugged her. She knew Mother was trying her best and she appreciated it.

"Is this a reception or a funeral?" Burt spoke up. "Let's eat."

Martha and Chrissy had taken care of the catering, and the dining area was filled with every sort of food choice imaginable. "Everything except turkey bacon!" Mother added as if she could read Sam's thoughts.

Sam laughed, and Ian stole another kiss. "So have you told Burt you're moving out yet?"

"I thought I'd let you tell him." He nuzzled the side of her neck.

"Coward."

"He's here at the wedding. You don't think he expects us to live separately, do you?"

"Of course not, but he might think we're going to continue to rent from him." Sam had planned for Ian to live with her above the diner. They hadn't really talked about it, but she'd just assumed. "If you're moving in with me, you should give him notice so he can rent out the studio to someone else."

He smiled against her neck as he squeezed her close. "So I'm moving into the apartment, boss? First I'm full-time cook, then business partner, now you tell me where I have to live. Am I even still on the payroll?"

Sam giggled as his lips tickled her neck. Eyes were on them, but she didn't care. "I supposed I could compensate you…in other ways."

The End

Thank you for reading Second Chance. Please consider spreading the word or posting a review on Amazon or Goodreads. Word of mouth is the nicest thing you can do for an author and very much appreciated.
Thank you,
Nancy Henderson

Other books by Nancy Henderson:
Shadow's Promise, historical romance
Four Winds, historical romance
Bounty, historical romance
Stranger in His Bed, historical romance
Blackbird, historical romance
Litterboxes and Hairballs: My Life with Cats, A collection of short humor stories about life and cat ownership

For a complete listing of Nancy's books, please visit her website at: http://www.always-a-story.com

Or her Amazon page:
http://www.amazon.com/Nancy-Henderson/e/B002BLZZZG/ref=ntt_dp_epwbk_0

Sign up for Nancy Henderson's newsletter and get updated on when new books come out! Click here to sign up: http://www.always-a-story.com

Made in the USA
Middletown, DE
21 September 2016